Tawny Weber

COMING ON STRONG

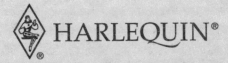

HARLEQUIN®

TORONTO • NEW YORK • LONDON
AMSTERDAM • PARIS • SYDNEY • HAMBURG
STOCKHOLM • ATHENS • TOKYO • MILAN • MADRID
PRAGUE • WARSAW • BUDAPEST • AUCKLAND

Recycling programs for this product may not exist in your area.

ISBN-13: 978-0-373-79466-9
ISBN-10:   0-373-79466-5

COMING ON STRONG

Copyright © 2009 by Tawny Weber.

ABOUT THE AUTHOR

Tawny Weber is usually found dreaming up stories in her California home, surrounded by dogs, cats and kids. When she's not writing hot, spicy stories for Harlequin Blaze, she's testing her latest margarita recipe, shopping for the perfect pair of boots or drooling over Johnny Depp pictures (when her husband isn't looking, of course). When she's not doing any of that, she spends her time scrapbooking and playing in the garden. She'd love to hear from readers, so drop by her home on the Web, www.TawnyWeber.com.

Books by Tawny Weber
HARLEQUIN BLAZE

Don't miss any of our special offers. Write to us at the following address for information on our newest releases.

Harlequin Reader Service
U.S.: 3010 Walden Ave., P.O. Box 1325, Buffalo, NY 14269
Canadian: P.O. Box 609, Fort Erie, Ont. L2A 5X3

To the Writers At Play:
Beth, Kath, Janice, Sheila, Anna, Kimmi,
Terri, Stacey, Carla, Betty, Marlene, Lisa, Trish,
Tammy, Heather, Angi, Leslie, Mona,
Anne-Marie, Cheryl and Terry.
Wild, crazy, amazing.
I love you all!

Prologue

"I DON'T THINK I can go through with it," Belle Forsham said, one hand pressed to her chest. Beneath the beaded silk of her bodice, her heart raced like a terrified rabbit. "I mean, this is crazy, you know? What the hell was I thinking?"

"If I recall, you were thinking that Mitch Carter was the hottest piece of ass you'd ever seen," Sierra Donovan said absently, her attention focused on getting the fluffy white tulle arranged just so over Belle's blonde curls.

"I said I *thought* he'd be the hottest piece of ass," Belle corrected, frowning at the image in the mirror. It was like watching herself through a Halloween filter. "I haven't been able to find out how hot he really is, though, have I? Which is why I'd be insane to go through with this, isn't it? Like, you know, buying a poked pig or something?"

"Pig in a poke?"

"Whatever."

Sierra just laughed and, with one last fluff of the veil, stepped back to gauge the results. "You look so…virginal."

Her best friend's tone said it all. Virginal was the last image Belle had ever aspired toward. Then again, she'd never figured on being a bride, either.

Wild and free, that was Belle's motto. Or it had been, right up until she'd met Mitch Carter. Then mottos had been nudged aside for her new obsession. Getting Mitch into bed.

Mitch was her daddy's new VP of development. The man was gorgeous. Rich auburn hair, cinnamon-brown eyes and the tightest butt she'd ever ogled. He exuded an energy that fascinated Belle. Power, definitely, and drive. A kind of intense focus that promised a woman that once she had his attention, he'd give her the most incredible sex of her life.

And Belle wanted his attention. But while she'd practically panted at his feet, he'd barely acknowledged her. For a woman used to men drooling on her buffed and polished toes, he'd been a total challenge. She threw herself at him, he gave her polite acknowledgment. She flirted, he watched. She pursued, he evaded.

Hard to get? Hell, Mitch Carter was damn near impossible.

At least, to get into bed. For some bizarre reason, after about a month of chasing him, he'd turned the tables. To use his own words, he'd started courting her. She smothered a baffled laugh at the idea of it. They'd mostly attended business functions, family events with her father, the occasional romantic dinner.

Unable to pace in the voluminous dress, Belle fidgeted on the stool where she sat. Her fingers fiddled with her late mother's pearl necklace, so sweetly innocent as it circled with a heavy weight of expectation around her neck. Like the white dress and delicate veil, the pearls really didn't suit her. Of course, neither did marriage.

Three months of dating. A smoking-hot kiss at the end of the evening. A little touchy-feely to add to the thrill. But never more. God, she'd wanted more. Then he'd scared the hell out of her when, out of the blue, he'd popped the question. Marriage. He wanted to make an honest woman of her…which was just plain weird since he hadn't tried her dishonest ways first.

She'd been so hot for him, she'd agreed instantly. She'd rushed the wedding plans, pulled out all the stops and organized a ritzy society event in less than three months. Through all the planning, something she'd proven to be amazingly skilled at, she'd had one thought and one thought only.

Hurry it up so she could get to her wedding night.

But now, when faced with the actual nuptials, she wasn't sure it was the right thing to do.

"Sierra, am I crazy to marry Mitch after only knowing him six months? I mean, is this too fast?"

Her friend opened her mouth, most likely to offer some dumb platitude about bridal jitters. It wasn't nerves, though. Belle didn't know what it was, but the lead weight in her stomach made her feel trapped, terrified. She'd much rather feel jittery anxiety instead.

Then Sierra shrugged, her own worry clear.

"I don't know," she admitted, chewing off her lipstick as she started to pace the room. Her typical in-your-face honesty and her maid-of-honor duty to keep Belle from freaking out were obviously at odds.

"Does it matter, though? You've wanted Mitch since you first saw him and now you're getting him. Long-term, even. You'll have killer sex tonight and blow his mind. Happy-ever-after, all that crap—that'll come with time."

Crap, indeed. The last thing anyone would call Belle was naive, but compared with the cynical Sierra she was a wide-eyed romantic. Whenever she thought past the honeymoon, let herself focus on anything besides the killer sex she was anticipating, she felt ill. She understood honeymoons. They were all about indulging in decadent sex in as many ways, places and times as possible. But marriage? Oh, God. She pressed her hand to her stomach, hoping she didn't get sick all over her dress. Was she ready to get married?

Belle stared at her reflection. White satin, seed beads and tulle. It all went perfectly with the pearls. Sweet and inno-cent. Definitely not her style. Her first choice for a dress had been sexy and edgy, but she'd thought Mitch would like this better.

"I guess that establishes why I'm marrying him," she said slowly. She loved him. Or, at least, she thought she did. Or, at least, she figured what she felt was probably love. She was fascinated by his kisses and his mind. By the sexual energy that simmered just under the surface. She was willing to make a promise to Mitch and keep it. Add to that the fact that she was agreeing to tie herself to the guy before he'd given her a single orgasm…well, that had to be love.

So, yes, she was ready for marriage.

"But why is he marrying me?" she asked in a whisper.

"Why don't you find out?" Sierra prompted for, like, the millionth time. "Quit second-guessing yourself and trying to please him and just ask."

Confront him? Straight up ask for possible rejection? Hell, no. One thing Belle had learned watching her late mother's bout with cancer was "what you don't know won't hurt you until later." She'd rather take her chances with the unknown.

"I'm just saying, if you want to know why Mitch is marrying you, he's the guy to ask," Sierra said, her tone making it obvious she knew she was wasting her breath.

"He's marrying you because he loves you, of course."

"What?" Surprised, she and Sierra both spun around to see Belle's other bridesmaid, Mitch's sister Lena.

Average height, average features, pale-brown hair cut in an unfortunate bob that did nothing to hide her very high forehead, Lena looked nothing like her brother. Belle had first met her when the woman had flown in from Pennsylvania a week earlier. Where Mitch was dynamic, Lena was tepid. It was hard to believe the two of them were even related.

Belle wanted to like her, but it was a struggle. She'd first suggested Lena join the wedding party in an attempt to make nice with Mitch's family. But the other woman had a mocking, judgmental air about her that grated on Belle's nerves. She was trying to ignore it, though. After all, this was her new sister-in-law.

"He must be madly in love with you," Lena pointed out as she inched into the room. The pale-rose bridesmaid dress that looked so sexy on Sierra made Lena look like a fluffy pink marshmallow. "Why else would he give up on his goals to get married?"

What goals was Mitch giving up? Belle gave Sierra a confused frown, then looked at Lena.

"Well, sure, partnership with your father is a huge incentive since Mitch had only planned on a short-term association with Forsham Hotels. It was the last step in his plan to take his construction company to the next level." She said all this while gliding an ugly shade of nutmeg lipstick over her thin lips. Then she met Belle's eyes in the mirror and shrugged. "His own development firm. He was counting on the experience and, you know, connections to help him out. Of course, I don't have to tell you how ambitious and determined to succeed he is."

"Partnership?" Belle frowned. What partnership?

"You didn't know?" Lena's mouth rounded to match the oops look in her brown eyes. "I'm so sorry. Maybe he was saving the news as a wedding surprise."

"He's a vice-president, not a partner," Sierra said, sounding as confused as Belle. "I thought he didn't have enough money or land to bring to the table for that kind of a deal."

"Well, yeah. But Uncle Danny said Mitch was given one of those offers he couldn't refuse. I guess your daddy's backing a risky land deal with the agreement that Mitch develop it for him. Aunt Edna said he saw a perfect opportunity and made the most of it." Lena gave a little who-knows shrug and a wide smile. Neither hid the malice peeking out from her simpering demeanor.

All those family names blurred in Belle's mind. She'd been

so excited to be a part of a large family, for the first time since she was eight to have more than just her and her dad at the Thanksgiving table. But after meeting Mitch's relatives, she wasn't so sure. It was like coming up against a very large, very cohesive wall. And she was on the wrong side of it.

Lena babbled more family gossip and inane insights into Mitch's personality. Belle just stared, her mind numb.

A risky land development? Her father wouldn't go into a project like that with just anyone. It would require a family commitment. Had he offered to make Mitch family? Or had Mitch offered to marry her in order to get the deal? And what did that make her? The price he had to pay for success? An easy route to the top?

Recognition, denial and sharp pain twisted together in her stomach. She'd wanted to believe he was marrying her because he couldn't resist, because he was crazy for her. But she'd obviously been wrong.

It all made sense now. His reluctance for intimacy, his emotional distance. Her earlier bridal jitters turned to cramping nausea. He was marrying his way into a business deal.

Lena's overarched brows drew together above her gleaming eyes. "You look a little green. Are you feeling okay?"

"Of course she's not," Sierra snapped. "What are you thinking, coming in here and spewing ugly rumors like that? What kind of person goes around gossiping about her brother on his wedding day?"

"Stepbrother," Lena corrected with a pout. "My dad married his mom when we were teenagers. And you're the nasty one. I was just saying that Belle's lucky that Mitch loves her enough to give up his dreams of his own development firm to work for her father. I wasn't insinuating anything else."

Lena wasn't his real sister? Why hadn't he told her? Belle didn't know why, but that was the last straw. She stood, the stool pressing against her full skirt like the bars on a cage. She wanted to run, but where? To Mitch? Hardly.

"The hell you weren't trying to cause trouble," Sierra growled at Lena. Their voices seemed to be coming from a long way away, muffled by the buzzing in Belle's head. "You're intimating that Belle's father bought her a groom. Like she or Mitch would be that desperate."

"Desperate? No. But when you put it that way, the wedding does sound a little fishy, doesn't it?" Lena gave them a wounded look, then headed for the door. Once there, she glanced over her shoulder. "Of course, I'm sure Belle knows Mitch loves her more than any silly promotion. I mean, who gets married without hearing vows of love? And Mitch never lies, not even for a business deal."

Sierra's cuss words hit Lena's retreating back. The brunette stormed to the door.

"Sierra," was all Belle said.

"I'm taking her down. That bitch isn't getting away with ruining your day."

For just one second, Belle let herself imagine Sierra jumping Lena and pummeling the smirk off her face. For the first time in her life, she considered diving in to help instead of yelling encouragement from the sidelines. Unlike her friend, Belle hated arguments.

Before she could decide whether or not to encourage Sierra to chase the woman's passive-aggressive ass down, Belle's father strode through the door. Handsome as ever in his tux, he winked at Sierra, then gave his only child a doting smile.

"You're a beautiful bride, sweetheart. Mitch is a lucky man."

Lucky? Really. It sounded like Mitch and her dad were the lucky ones. After all, they'd made the deal between them. She felt like the booby prize. She sucked in a shuddering breath, trying to calm the nausea rolling through her system. It would be so easy to just go through with this. She wasn't stupid. She'd known Mitch didn't love her. She wasn't sure she loved him, although she'd been willing to convince herself she did. But, like this stupid school-girl wedding dress, she'd been trying to give him whatever he wanted. And he couldn't even give her the truth?

Tears stung her eyes as she mentally kissed happy-ever-after, *and all that crap,* goodbye. Which didn't suck nearly as much as being cheated out of her wedding night.

Belle swallowed hard and looked into the face of the only man she'd ever felt safe loving. "Daddy? Did you offer to make Mitch your partner?"

Oblivious as usual to his daughter's emotional state, Franklin Forsham shrugged and patted her shoulder. "Not to worry, sweetie. I won't work him too hard."

Belle's gaze met Sierra's. Sympathetic tears washed away the anger in her friend's vivid blue eyes.

Numb now, Belle looked past her father's broad shoulders through the open door to the archway leading to the chapel. She could see the swags of orchids and pink roses, hear the soft tones of the harp. Her storybook wedding awaited.

She couldn't do it. She wasn't a negotiating point or a piece of property to be acquired in a business deal.

"I can't go through with the wedding," she declared, gathering the slick folds of her white satin skirt in her fist. "I won't sell myself. I might be willing to change, to compromise, but I draw the line at being lied to and cheated."

"What are you talking about?" Franklin's face turned white, then red. Hands clenched, he looked like he wanted to hit someone. "Mitch cheated on you?"

Scared of the anger on her father's face, of the pain pouring through her, Belle just shrugged. Cheated on her, cheated her, what was the difference? Emotion choked her, heated tears washed down her cheeks. Unable to hold back her sobs, she threw herself into her father's arms.

This was the last time she'd ever let a man, or the promise of hot sex, mean a damned thing to her.

1

Six years later

"I FOUND a replacement for Gloria, Mr. Carter. Everyone says this is the best event planner on the west coast."

Unspoken was the understanding that Mitch would accept nothing less than the best. Which was difficult, considering his luxury resort was six weeks from opening to the public and had been beset by one problem after another. The most recent was the loss of the woman he'd contracted to handle all the resort events.

"Call me Mitch," he absently told his new assistant. He motioned to the vacant seat opposite his desk, but she shook her head, preferring to stand.

She'd been here a couple of weeks, but Diana was still jumpy and nervous. He knew he was demanding of his employees and it definitely made it easier to demand if they were on a first-name basis, so she'd better get over her timidity soon. They were almost at the end of his Mr. Nice Guy two-week break-in period.

He took the papers she handed him and in one glance was thrown back in time. Shocked, Mitch stared at the glossy dossier. The black-and-white photo didn't do justice to Belle Forsham's fairy-like beauty. It didn't capture the gleam of her tousled blond curls, or the wicked tilt of her sea-green eyes. The shadows accented her sharp features, the light reflecting off her smile.

The best? Yeah, she was. Good enough to make a man stupid. He glared at that smile, irritated with his body's reaction. Belle Forsham was pure trouble. He knew she was, and still he got hard remembering the taste of her lips. He tried to dull his body's reaction by visualizing himself standing, alone, at the altar.

Yeah, the anger definitely dimmed his desire.

"Mr. Carter?" Diana interrupted his pathetic obsessing. "Do you want me to contact Eventfully Yours? They're perfect for the job given the scope of the resort's needs and what you are looking for in an event planner."

"I'd rather not work with this particular company," he said, making it sound like he'd put some thought into the decision. In reality, no thought was required. Despite how often she showed up in his dreams, usually nude, Belle was at the bottom of the list of women he wanted to see. And she was definitely the last one he'd consider depending on for any aspect of his success.

After all, who knew better just how undependable she was? He tossed the file on the pile on his desk, the banner on her dossier catching his eye. He sneered. *Society's Planning Princess,* indeed.

"But…I don't understand. Everyone says they're the best. They've worked for a dozen A-list actors, some of the top musicians in the country and any number of politicians. They've arranged club openings, publisher parties, award-ceremony after-parties."

"They're not what I'm looking for," he snapped.

Diana's face fell, making her look like a sad chipmunk. Obviously sticking with her own version of the dress-for-success theory, she wore a tidy suit, stockings and ugly shoes. The overall image was serious efficiency, which was supported by the fact that she did a damned good job. Mitch wouldn't have hired her otherwise. He just wished she'd loosen up. He glanced down at his own jeans and workboots and gave a mental shrug. So she didn't have to loosen up to his level, but a little less formality wouldn't hurt.

"Let's look at the other event planners," Mitch instructed. "Sometimes a reputation is based on perception, rather than how good the firm actually is. I need more than gloss to make this work. If Lakeside is going to succeed, I'm going to need clever, resourceful and intuitive."

He pushed away from his overloaded desk and strode to the wide bank of windows that looked out to the lake. Almost completed, this resort was the culmination of all his dreams. Ten acres of verdant hills, lush gardens and what he secretly referred to as the enchanted forest, Lakeside was going to be the brightest jewel in his development crown and his first venture into hotels. So far he'd launched a half-dozen business parks, a mall and a couple of small restaurants. All of which he'd turned for a sweet profit.

But this resort was more than ambitious. For a guy who'd started out swinging a hammer, it was a huge coup. To kick this venture off here, in Southern California, was ballsy, given that he'd torched his bridges with the top hotelier on the west coast six years ago.

"I need a creative wizard with killer contacts. Someone who gets what our clientele will want, who can make the resort a posh getaway for the wealthy. If I'm going to turn this into the most talked-about hot spot of the rich and famous, I'm going to need someone who kicks ass."

Diana's mouth worked for a second, then after an obvious internal struggle, she thrust out her chin and pointed to the abandoned dossier on his desk.

"But that's what I've been trying to tell you, *Mitch*. Belle Forsham is all of that. Her events are the most talked-about, the most outside-the-box successes of the last two years. She seems to know everyone, do everything. She…" Diana stopped, wrinkled her nose and took a deep breath before continuing. "She kicks ass."

Amazed she'd finally used his given name, Mitch gave a snort of laughter at the uptight way she said *ass*. Amusement faded as he glanced again at the photo of his ex-fiancée.

When had she gone into event planning? And how the hell had she stuck with it long enough to be such a success? He had to admit, though, she had the intelligence and creativity to make it happen, although she'd always tried to hide the brains behind a flirty flutter of her lashes. She was definitely a social butterfly. He recalled the guest list for their aborted wedding. It had read like the who's who of *People* magazine.

It was the memory of that damned wedding, the humiliation of standing alone in front of all those gawking and snickering witnesses, that cinched it. Mitch ground his teeth, long-simmering anger burning in his gut. Belle might have great ideas, be clever and well-connected. But when the chips were down, she couldn't be counted on.

"She's a flake," he finally said.

"She's the best." Diana held up a sheaf of papers, all recommending Eventfully Yours. "Everything I've heard, all the research I did says that Belle Forsham is the It Girl of events. She's the hottest thing on the west coast."

Ambition fought with ego. The good of his company versus the biggest humiliation of his past. His need to see Belle again, to see if she was still that intriguing combination of sexy and sweet, battled with his desire to keep the door to that part of his history nailed shut.

Mitch looked over the resort grounds again, the gentle beauty of the sun-gilded lake beckoning him. Reminding him to do his best. A lot was riding on this deal. He'd sunk all his available resources into making this resort the most luxurious, the most welcoming. None of that would matter without guests with big enough wallets to indulge themselves.

He'd screwed himself into a corner once because of Belle Forsham. Or because of his desire to screw her, to be exact. He'd never wanted a woman the way he'd wanted Belle. But she'd been his boss's only child and off-limits. His old-fashioned upbringing and his worry that he'd be disrespecting Franklin if he had wild monkey sex with the guy's daughter had inspired him to the dumbest proposal of his life. Well, that and his idiotic belief that he'd fallen in love with her.

He'd handled it all wrong. He could see that now, but that didn't change the fact that she'd dumped him at the altar, and because of her he'd lost both his job and the respect of his mentor. Which bothered him almost as much as never having the wild Belle-against-the-wall sex he'd wanted so badly.

And he was supposed to welcome her back in his life? Was he willing to make a deal with the sexiest little devil he'd ever known in order to ensure his success?

He thought of his team. They were just as invested in the resort as he was. Because Mitch had little experience in the resort business, he'd brought in two managers—one to oversee the hotel, the other to run the three restaurants. He was the money man, the one with the vision, but he needed each of them on board to handle the hundred-plus employees and make sure the day to day of the operation ran smoothly while he made his vision a reality.

He glanced at the family picture behind his desk. He knew his family took great pride in his accomplishments, just as they had huge expectations for his success. Expectations that included supporting his grandmother and providing jobs for four of his cousins in his company. Those expectations were both a source of pride and a noose around his neck. He had to succeed.

The resort already had enough problems. On top of the usual

construction glitches and startup issues, they'd been having a run of bad luck. Losing his event coordinator was just the last in a long string of unexplained setbacks. Could he afford to blow off the perfect planner out of pride?

Damn. He sighed and pushed the file on the desk toward Diana.

"Check her availability."

"THERE'S ONLY one man who'll satisfy you. Quit stalling and go for it, already."

Belle Forsham stopped pacing across the lush amethyst carpet of her office to roll her eyes at her best friend and business partner. The office was a quirky combination of trendy accessories, sexy textures and practical lines. Much like Belle herself.

"It's not like chasing some guy down for hot sex, Sierra. This is serious. We're talking business here. My father's business. Or should I say, the end of my father's business."

"Exactly. You want to save Forsham Hotels, you need to get help." Sierra flipped open the pink bakery box she'd brought in for their morning meeting and, after a careful perusal, chose a carrot-cheesecake muffin.

Not even looking at the other offerings, Belle automatically went for the fanciest muffin. Rich, chocolaty and decadent, just the way she liked it. Except she was so stressed, she put it down after one bite. Why waste the indulgence?

"I don't need help," she lied.

"Yes, you do. It's not like you and I can plan an event that will save your dad's butt," Sierra shot back, referring to their company, Eventfully Yours, as she licked cream-cheese icing from her thumb.

They were *the* elite event planners on the west coast, catering to the rich and famous from southern California up to Monterey. Combining Sierra's fearless attitude and Belle's knack for creative entertainment, the two women had hit the Hollywood scene hard and strong four years back. Eventfully Yours had grown from organizing themed play dates for sitcom divas' Pomeranians to arranging intimate soirees for A-list actors and five hundred of their closest friends.

"You know, now that I think about it, I really shouldn't be going behind my father's back," Belle stalled, sitting on the edge of her inlaid rosewood desk. "He'd be the first to say his heart attack is no reason to treat him like an invalid. If he wanted to make a deal to save the hotels, he'd do it himself."

Used to Belle's habit of squirreling out of anything that made her uncomfortable, Sierra just stared. It was that uncompromising, see-all-the-way-into-her-soul look that Belle hated. Whenever Sierra narrowed her blue eyes and shot her that look, Belle felt like a total wuss.

"Don't you think if my dad wanted to deal with Mitch Carter, he'd approach him himself?" she asked, playing her last excuse.

"Right. Your dad, upstanding guy that he is, is gonna go begging help from the man he fired from a dream VP position and partnership in one of the primo hotel conglomerates in the U.S. The same guy his daughter ditched at the altar."

"Exactly," Belle exclaimed, jumping up from her perch on the desk to throw her arms in the air. "Given our sucky history, why would you think Mitch wants anything to do with me?"

Sierra arched a brow, then gave a little shrug. Taking her time, she dusted the crumbs off her fingers, shifted in the plush chair and curled her long legs under her. Raising one brow, she tapped a manicured nail on her bare ankle.

"This is the guy who refused to have sex with you before marriage. I figure he has some twisted belief in things like honor."

Sierra rolled her eyes at her own words. Always the cynic, she didn't understand the concept of selfless honor. Of course, neither did Belle. But it sure sounded sweet.

"This would also be the same guy who, despite having the perfect opportunity to make your daddy's life a living hell when you ruined their deal, simply shook hands and walked away."

Walked away and left her daddy holding a piece of investment property that, because of zoning and development legalities, was now taking his business down the toilet. But considering what Belle had done, that wasn't really Mitch's fault. Was it?

"So he's freaking hero material," she muttered. "So what?"

Belle slid off her heels so she could pace faster. Nothing slowed down a good pace like four-inch Manolos. The way her luck was running, she'd stumble and break the heel. And she needed to move around and try to shake off the nasty feeling that had settled over her when she'd been reminded of how badly she'd treated Mitch. That he'd broken her heart was no excuse. She knew that now. But knowing it and being willing to do something about it were definitely two different things.

"Exactly," Sierra agreed. "He's hero material. Which means he's hard-wired to ride to the rescue. Even after all that crap went down, Mitch never badmouthed you or your father. If he knew how bad things are now, maybe he'd offer some advice. Or best case? He'll step in, checkbook at the ready, and save the company."

Belle grimaced.

Mitch definitely lived by his own code. Over the last six years he'd developed a reputation as the man with the magic touch. Mr. Money, a real-estate developer with an eye for success, he was known in the industry as a fair man who played by his own rules, uncompromising, intense and dynamic. People appreciated his generous willingness to share his success, but behind the scenes, there were whispers of ruthless payback to anyone who crossed him.

Which didn't bode well for Belle, since she was the one seen as most deserving of Mitch's revenge. Mutual acquaintances still joked that she'd better watch her back. She knew better, though. She'd never mattered enough to him to merit that much attention.

"He won't deal with me," she assured Sierra, playing her trump card.

"You don't know that." The way Sierra said it, as though she had some naughty little secret, made Belle nervous.

"Yes, I do." Belle took a deep breath and, with the air of one confessing a mortal sin, dropped her voice to a loud whisper. "I never told you, but I tried to see Mitch. Two years ago. Remember when I had that car wreck?"

Eyes huge with curiosity, Sierra nodded.

"I was shook up and had some weird idea that being hit in a head-on accident on a one-way street was a sign that I should make amends for all my wicked ways." She met her friend's snort of laughter with a glare. "I figured ditching Mitch topped my wicked list, so I sucked up my courage and went to apologize."

"No way," Sierra breathed. "And you didn't tell me?"

"There was nothing to tell. He was supposedly out of the country."

"Supposedly?"

"Well, I went back a couple weeks later and his assistant said he was out with the flu."

"So?"

"So isn't it obvious? He was avoiding me."

"He left the country and got the flu to avoid you?"

Belle rolled her eyes. "No, that was just BS. He was probably there in his office telling his assistant to make something up so he didn't have to see me."

Sierra's expression clearly said "you've got to be kidding."

"Don't give me that look. It could be true."

"Only if the roles were reversed. You're the one afraid of confrontation, Belle. Not Mitch. If he were in the office, I'm sure he'd have taken five minutes to personally tell you to kiss his ass."

"And you want me to go chasing the guy for favors?" Belle ignored the confrontation issue. It was true, after all. "We both know he doesn't want anything to do with me."

Sierra hummed, then slid off the chair and crossed to the leather bag she'd tossed on the credenza. She pulled out a file folder with what looked like a printout of an e-mail clipped to it.

Waving the file at Belle, she arched a brow and asked, "Wanna bet?"

"Spill," Belle demanded, making a grab for the folder. Sierra whipped it out of reach with a laugh.

"You really need to have more faith in your impact on people."

"According to you, people are only out for what they can get," Belle shot back.

"Exactly. So while Mitch might happily punish you when it's convenient, the tune changes when he needs something."

"And he needs us?"

"No. He needs you. This gig is right up your alley," Sierra claimed. Which meant it was totally social. Sierra handled the big corporate and studio events, the types of things that required juggling numbers, working with specific images or ground rules. In other words, the more traditional events that relied heavily on organization. Belle's specialty was the over-the-top hedonistic fantasies. And since she'd indulged in so many fantasies about Mitch Carter, the idea of having another shot at sharing a few with him sent her pulse racing.

"Spill," she demanded. She tried to ignore the excitement dancing in her stomach, making her edgy and impatient. This was crazy. Mitch hated her. He had to. But maybe, just maybe, this was her shot at making amends. At fixing the past and helping her father. And maybe, just maybe…at finally getting into his pants.

She'd blown it before, stumbling over that silly marriage idea. But she was older and much more experienced now. This time she'd be smarter. If she and Mitch did find common ground, all she wanted was sex. That, and help for her dad.

She took the file from Sierra with a smile of anticipation. Belle read the e-mail. Then she read it again. The excitement curdled in her stomach.

"A resort grand opening? That's more your gig than mine," Belle said, trying to ignore the disappointment that settled over her like an itchy wool blanket.

"That's what they say they want. But check out the details I found."

Knowing her friend's instincts were usually spot-on, Belle opened the file. It just took a glance, a quick flip through the papers and plans for her to see the perfect hook to turn his lush resort into the hottest, most exclusive getaway on the west coast.

Mitch's background was in development. And he was damned good at it. But he was thinking too traditionally for this resort. It wasn't a run-of-the-mill hotel and shouldn't be treated that way. Given the remote beauty of the location, yet its easy access to L.A., it could be the nice luxury vacation place he had outlined. Or it could be the chicest spot for decadence in southern California. Indulgent weekends, clandestine trysts, decadent fantasies. All there, for a price. All guaranteed to be unique, elite and, best of all, private.

Her blood heated, ideas flashing like strobe lights through her mind. Excitement buzzed, but she tried to tamp it down. There was nothing worse than getting all stirred up, only to be left flat. It was like foreplay with no orgasm. Amusing once or twice, but ultimately a rip-off.

"This e-mail isn't from Mitch himself," she pointed out. "And his assistant isn't offering us the position, she's only checking availability."

"So? Since when have we waited for an engraved invitation to charm our way into a job?"

Good point. The two women had spent their first year in business clubbing and hitting every social event they could wiggle or charm their way into on the off chance of finding clients. Once at a fashion show someone had mentioned a director's wife with a penchant for poodles and Motown. The next day Belle contacted the director and suggested he throw his wife a surprise party, with the musical dog theme. Such ballsiness paid off both in contacts and jobs as they'd built Eventfully Yours.

But this was different. Mitch probably hated her. Then again, why would he be willing to work with her if he was holding a grudge? Belle sighed, not sure if her reasoning was sound or pure bullshit.

"We have an opportunity to kick ourselves to the next level with a job this exclusive," Sierra said quietly as she settled back in her chair. "Better yet, you have a chance here to settle up some past debts, get some of that fabled closure. Are you going to let semantics stop you?"

Was she? Belle glanced at Sierra, noting the assured confidence on her friend's angular face. Sierra wouldn't push unless she thought it was really important. She might be a relentless nag when it came to the success of Eventfully Yours. But she was a good friend and would never sacrifice Belle to snag a client. Even one as potentially huge as MC Development.

Belle had spent the last six years regretting her screw-up. She should have faced Mitch herself instead of running like a wuss. Hell, she should never have agreed to marriage in the first place. She'd known better. Sex, as incredible as it might have been, was no reason to go off the deep end. But she'd been afraid to push the issue, then after the altar-ditch, too hurt and upset to face his anger.

Ever since, she'd tried to find a guy to replace him, both in her bed and her fantasies. None had stuck, though. Probably because she'd never actually had Mitch. This might be her chance to get over him, once and for all.

She glanced back at the files, the panoramic photo of the resort and its welcoming lakeside forest. She wanted to see it in person. Even more, she wanted to do Mitch, right there on the edge of that lake. Outdoor sex in the woods, like something out of a fairy tale. The orgasm she was imagining was probably mythical, too. But she didn't care. She wanted to find out.

Despite the nerves clawing at her, she set the file down, slipped her shoes on and grabbed her purse.

"Shopping?" Sierra asked, sliding her feet into her shoes, too.

"We'll start with lingerie. I heard about this new place called Twisted Knickers. The designs supposedly take provocative to a whole new level."

FOCUSED ON his conversation, Mitch strode past Diana's desk with his cell phone glued to his ear. His assistant waved her hand, trying to get his attention, but he held up one finger, then pointed to his office door. He'd talk to her when he was done.

"I don't want any more excuses," Mitch ordered his foreman. "The electrical has to be finished by the first of the month." This damned week had gone downhill fast. There'd been even more building delays, his designer had gone into labor two months early, and now electrical problems. To top it off, he'd talked to three event planners so far and none had come close to sparking his interest. He was wound so tight, he was ready to snap. "The plumbing is already three weeks behind. If we lose any more ground, we won't open on schedule. If that happens, we're screwed."

He listened to his foreman's justifications with half an ear as, still ignoring Diana's increasingly frantic gestures, he opened his office door. As always, the view of the lush green woods through the window beckoned him. Maybe he'd go for a run, shake off some of the tension. He'd rather have a long, sweaty roll in the sheets, but he couldn't afford the distraction. Not when everything was on the line.

One more step into his office and Mitch felt like he'd been hit in the face. Maybe it was sex on the brain, but even the air shifted, turning sultry and suggestive. He breathed in, his lungs filling with a musky floral scent.

Instant turn-on.

Seated as she was in the high-backed leather chair facing the window, all Mitch could see were long, sexy legs ending in strappy black do-me heels. He tried to swallow, but his mouth had gone dirt-dry. Those were wrap-around-the-shoulders-and-ride-'em-wild legs.

Damn. Talk about distraction.

Mitch flipped his phone closed, not sure if he'd said goodbye or even if his foreman was still talking. He stepped further into the office, deliberately closing the door behind him. Two more steps into the room, and he could see around the high leather back of the chair.

Gorgeous. The impact was like getting kicked in the gut by a black belt on steroids. Swift, intense and indefensible. The first time he'd seen Belle, she'd been twenty-one. He'd thought then she couldn't possibly be more confident in her own sexual power. He'd obviously been wrong, since she was now a master of it. Or was that mistress? And why did that make him crave studded black leather shorts?

Six years had added layers of polish, maturity and assurance to her already powerful sexual charisma. Mitch's gaze reluctantly left those delicious legs to travel upward. He noted the flirty green skirt, the same shade as her eyes, ending a few inches above her knees. A wide leather belt accented her waist and emphasized her lush breasts in the gossamer soft-white blouse. Mitch let his eyes rest there for just a second, millions of regrets pounding in his head. He wished like hell that once, just once, he'd tasted their bounty.

He was sure if he had, he'd have easily kept her out of his mind. The only reason he'd never found another woman to replace her was that he'd blown the fantasy of sex between them all out of proportion.

He felt her amusement before he even looked at her face. Belle was used to being ogled, so he didn't waste time on embarrassment. He wondered briefly at giving her that much power this early in the game, but he couldn't seem to help himself. That there was a game afoot was implicit. The question wasn't who would win, either. It was how much it would cost him to play.

She arched one platinum brow, amused challenge clear in her eyes and the dimple that played at the corner of her full lips. Her hair was shorter now, angled to emphasize her rounded cheekbones and the sharp line of her jaw.

"Well, well," Mitch drawled, moving around to lean on his desk while he faced the biggest mistake of his life. "If it isn't my long-lost bride."

2

"LONG-LOST bride-*to-be,* if you please," Belle corrected precisely.

She had to work to keep her smile in place. As much as she'd have preferred to avoid reference to their past, she'd known Mitch, for all his gentlemanly reputation, wouldn't sidestep the issue. She took a little breath before she lifted her chin. Since she had to deal with it, she'd face it head-on.

Or at least make him think she was dealing with it just long enough to flirt her way off the topic.

"Don't you look gorgeous," she commented with a wink. Since he'd made no attempt to hide his visual tour, she let her eyes take their own leisurely stroll, appreciating the view from head to toe.

Damn, he really had gotten better with age. His hair, still that deliciously rich auburn, was a little longer, a little less formal. His face was leaner, his shoulders broader. She was tempted to ask him to turn around so she could decide if his ass was any tighter. But it was awfully hard to beat perfection, so she doubted it.

"The years have definitely treated you well, Mitch."

Beneath her husky words and confident smile, her insides felt as though they were on a wobbly roller coaster. Despite that, she slid to her feet in one slow, sensual motion. His cinnamon-brown eyes blurred as she stepped forward. Heat flared between them, the same heat that had lured her from interested to obsessive so long ago.

Then, so quickly she wondered if she'd imagined the desire, he blinked and the look switched to simple curiosity. Belle had to fight to keep her smile in place. Damn him, that's how he'd always twisted her into knots. One second she'd been sure he was hot for her, the next he had total control.

Not this time.

Instead of the expected move, another step closer so she was in body-heat distance of him, Belle shifted her weight. Her hip to one side, she lifted a shoulder and gave a flutter of her lashes.

"Well?" she asked.

Mitch just arched one brow. His shoulders, she noted, were stiff, as though he was preparing himself. For what? she wondered. A handshake, a hug or, even worse, a big sloppy kiss.

She was tempted. But lurking behind that polite curiosity in his eyes was something edgier. Perhaps he was just waiting to verbally rip into her. Instead of intimidating her, that just added to the excitement.

"Well, what?"

Some insane impulse urged Belle to blurt out an apology. To tell him how sorry she was for the pain she must have caused. To confess her immaturity, her lack of consideration. Luckily, nerves trapped the words in her throat.

"Did you miss me?" she asked instead. Getting Mitch to deal with her, to give her the contract and with it the opening to butter him up so he'd help her father, was going to be hard enough. Why throw fuel on the flames? Especially when she was much more interested in starting a whole new fire.

"About as much as I miss the Macarena," he shot back.

Belle snickered. Then, unable to help herself, she laid her hand on his forearm. "It is good to see you again."

Eyes narrowed, he glanced down at her hand, then back at

her face. With a shrug, he gave a half smile and jerk of his chin. Only an optimist would call it a nod. Belle, being a glass-half-full kind of gal, took heart.

"Why are you here?"

"Right to the point, hmm?" Belle used the seconds it took her to return to her seat to take a deep breath. Control was crucial here. She had to play it just right.

With that in mind, she leaned back against the soft leather and gave Mitch a warm smile.

"I've got something you need," she told him.

"I'll pass," he responded instantly. "I tried to get it once before and look how that worked out."

Belle hid her wince. Whether the pain in her chest was from a singed ego or her bruised heart she didn't know.

"Maybe you were using the wrong inducement."

"Obviously," he said. Apparently resigned to the fact that she wasn't going to explain her presence until she was good and ready, he moved around his desk to take a seat.

"Oh, please. Let's be realistic. I was young and hot for you. For what I imagined would be incredible sex between the two of us. I wasn't looking for marriage, but that was the price you put on yourself." Talk about role reversal. She might be a jerk for her way of handling the situation, but he was a bigger jerk for being willing to use *her* lust to advance *his* career. But if she wasn't holding any grudges, why should he? "We'd have been much better off if you'd just gone for the kinky affair I was hoping for instead of insisting on milking the free cow."

"Why buy the cow if you can get the milk for free," he corrected.

"There you go," she said with a smile. "Except we were both after something other than milk, weren't we?"

She'd wanted sex, he'd wanted a foot up the career ladder. Neither one of them came off lily-pure, so she didn't bother pointing that out. Instead, she leaned down to pull a file out of her black leather portfolio.

"I understand you need an event planner."

Mitch's jaw tightened, but he just gave a dismissive shrug. His shirt rippled over arms that looked very intriguing. She'd bet there were some sweet biceps under that pristine cotton. Her teeth itched to take a nibble and see just how hard his muscle was.

"I might have considered a planner for the grand opening, but I'm not overly attached to the concept," he hedged.

Which meant he wanted one, he just didn't want it to be her. No problem. She'd change his mind.

"That's smart," she said, leaving the file in her lap instead of handing it to him. "Your grand opening should make a statement, of course. But you want that message to integrate with Lakeside's theme, its purpose."

"This isn't Disneyland," he pointed out, rolling his eyes.

"No, but you would do well to look at the success of theme parks like that. They have a clear message. A purpose that fulfils the guests' specific needs. Everything they offer, every single thing, supports that purpose."

"My resort has a purpose. You grew up in the hotel business, you already know this."

"But you're not trying to launch a hotel here, are you? You aren't targeting the average vacationer, honeymoon couple or getaway guest."

"I'm not?"

Even though he phrased it as a question, his tone was pure let's-humor-the-airhead. She was used to people taking one look at her blond hair and sexy image and judging her by stereotypes. Since it usually worked to her advantage, Belle didn't mind. At least, she told herself she didn't. It wasn't like Mitch knew her well enough to understand her or anything. So she fell into her typical lure-'em-in-and-close-the-deal mode with a flutter of her lashes.

"Are you? What do you see this resort offering?" she asked off-handedly.

"Offering? What any resort offers, of course. First-class luxury accommodations. Relaxation and pampering. The perfect getaway."

"I can get luxury and pampering at my father's hotels for half the price," she pointed out.

His eyes flashed at the mention of her father. Uh-oh, not a good sign. But instead of commenting, he just pointed out the window.

"Not with this lavish view, prime location or decadent opulence. Lakeside is top of the line. Luxurious suites, each with its own fireplace and bar. Three-hundred-count Egyptian sheets and down comforters, one-of-a-kind artwork and a stunning view from every room. We have the hottest golf course, three four-star restaurants, a ballroom, spa, designer shops."

Belle pressed her lips together to hide the smile brought on by his fervent recital of his resort's brochure. He sounded like a momma defending her baby against the crime of mediocrity. Good, that meant he was heavily invested in making Lakeside the biggest success possible.

"Let's cut to the chase, hmm?" she said once she was sure she could keep the triumph from her tone. "To really make your resort stand out, to make it a certifiable success, you need a hook. If you want the wealthy southern California clientele to flock here like flaming moths you're going to need to offer something a little more exotic than nice sheets, a golf course and hot stone massages."

"Moths to a flame," he corrected.

"Exactly," she agreed with a wink. "And like those moths, the wealthy and famous will swarm here. With the right incentive, of course."

"What do you have in mind?" he asked, sounding reluctantly intrigued. His gaze fell to the papers in her lap.

She tapped one red-tipped fingernail on the file and smiled.

"To use that Disney analogy again, I'm talking about a theme park for adults. Wealthy adults. Or better yet, famous wealthy adults. Ones who are looking for a grown-up park to play in."

Belle leaned forward to put the file on his desk. Mitch's gaze dropped to her cleavage. From the heat in his eyes, the way they went dark and intense, she figured her Twisted Knickers leather-and-lace demi-bra had just paid off.

"You want to make this resort a standout, you need to cater to the rich and famous. If you want them lining up to get in here, you need to offer them the one thing they want more than anything else. The one thing they'd pay almost any price for."

Keeping his eyes locked on hers, Mitch used one finger to pull the file toward him. He didn't flip it open, but sat there with his hand over it as if considering whether it was even worth the effort.

"And that is?" he finally asked.

"Sex, of course."

MITCH'S JAW dropped. This was a multimillion dollar venture, prime real estate, and he had everything on the line—his money, his company and, even more important, his reputation.

"You're suggesting I turn my luxury resort into a sex club?"

He didn't know why the idea surprised him. Everything about Belle made him think of sex. It always had. From her husky voice to her bedroom eyes and on down that gorgeous body to her suckable toes.

But he'd screwed up his career once because he'd been obsessed with her. Blinded by the dream of having it all, he'd tossed aside his own plans to accommodate her and her father's wishes, and ended up with nothing. It'd taken him three years to rebuild his reputation, another two to regain lost ground. He wasn't about to screw up again.

"Actually, I doubt you'd be able to pull off the sex club," she replied with a long look that made it clear she'd love to see him try. "There are some fabulous ones around that make good money, of course, but that's not quite the niche I had in mind."

It took physical effort to keep himself from asking her just how familiar she was with these *fabulous* sex clubs. He managed, just barely, to smother the biting jealousy that clawed at his gut when he imagined her hitting those clubs with another man. Or, given the clubs, other *men*.

Dammit, six years ago, that ugly green monster had goaded him into proposing marriage instead of taking her up on the wild sexual affair she'd offered. He hated—not just disliked, but viciously rip-the-head-off-whoever-it-was hated—the idea of some other man touching Belle. She was the only woman in the world to inspire him to want to brand her. To make her his and his alone, in every way possible. For a man who considered himself evolved beyond caveman idiocy, it had been a blow to the ego. Not enough of a blow to stun the jealousy monster, though.

To distract himself from the images, and from the memory of her lush, lace-clad breasts, clearly visible when she'd leaned across to hand him the file, Mitch tilted his head in question.

"What exactly are you proposing?"

"Private sex," she said in the same tone she'd use to share a national secret.

"Huh?" He didn't get it. The rooms had locks. There were no video cameras around.

"The paparazzi and gossip hounds have declared open season on celebrities. They have no degree of privacy anymore. Not only actors and musicians, but any big name in the industry. Before you relocated here, you were based in New York, right?" At his nod, she continued, "You probably see it, or would if you paid attention, on the east coast. But it's nothing like the insanity here in southern California."

"What does that have to do with sex? Or, how did you put it? Private sex?"

Belle arched one brow. "Everything. Haven't you ever wanted some hot, wild getaway sex at a luxury resort?"

Hell, yeah. He wanted it now, as a matter of fact. Mitch did a quick mental tally of how many bedrooms were complete here at the resort. He could do Belle in fourteen hot, wild ways without using the same room twice. Even more if they went vertical. And that wasn't even counting the private cottages scattered around the resort grounds.

"Your rich and famous are welcome to come have sex here," he told her. "We're an equal-opportunity resort in that regard."

Her look made him laugh. Like a crack in her perfect image, she went from glossy sex kitten to cute and adorable in the wrinkle of her nose.

"I'm glad to know you have no restrictions on sex," she responded, her tone husky and blatantly interested. "I hope that applies to your personal life as well as your resort?"

"The only restriction I follow is to avoid trouble." His grin fell away as he remembered that Belle was pure trouble, inside and out.

She tut-tutted. "Safe sex? How boring is that? The only time those two words belong together is in reference to health precautions."

Images of swings, leather and handcuffs—without the cushy fur lining—flashed through his mind. His body stirred in instant reaction. Damn, maybe he needed to rethink this keeping-Belle-at-a-distance thing? After all, she was here, he was here. They had no commitment beyond the moment, were free to do as they liked. Maybe instead of cursing the past, he should take her up on the offer of pleasure so clear in her eyes.

Fourteen rooms.

Wild sex.

Handcuffs.

And then show her on her way.

"I take it you'd rather have unsafe sex?" he asked with a slow, teasing smile. Mentally watching his caution trampled by lust, Mitch waved good-bye to good sense and gave Belle a look that said just how unsafe he'd like sex to get between them.

Her expression didn't change, but a faint flush washed over her chest, letting him know she wasn't unaffected. His mouth watered to taste her there, just above the curve of her breasts. The rational, ambitious voice in his head warned him not to get dragged down by his dick. She was trouble. She'd proved that by almost ruining him when she'd walked out. His dick didn't give a damn.

"I like sex," she corrected, "without rules and restrictions."

"I like the sound of that. Tell me more."

"What I really want is a chance to show you."

Rock-hard and ready to sweep his desk clean for a hot, fast preview, Mitch bit back a groan. Principles fought lust. Need smothered angst.

Then Belle stood, took two short steps to his desk and leaned forward. One leg bent, she rested her knee and hip on the desk. Right there on the redwood surface where he'd just fantasized about stripping her bare.

Her scent, something that reminded him of a moonlit garden on a hot summer night, wrapped around him with long, delicate fingers. When she leaned closer, it was all he could do to keep from grabbing her. Better to let her make the move, he told himself. Less liability for going along than for doing the grabbing. He swallowed, his mouth ready to taste her, his tongue craving the feel of hers.

Inches away, she stopped. Mitch frowned. No kiss?

She arched one brow, then tilted her head to indicate the file lying on the desk between them. Of course. He snickered at himself, a mocking reminder that this woman was trouble.

A sardonic smile curving his lips, he took the hint and flipped open the file. Might as well give it a cursory glance so he could refuse her services before they got horizontal.

It didn't take long for Mitch to take in the file contents. Event outlines, yes. But more than just party ideas, the proposal included a general marketing plan and focus strategy.

A chill ran up his back when Mitch skimmed the vision statement. Either she was a hell of a lot savvier than he gave her credit for or she had an inside track to his company's information. Because this statement was the twin of his own, with a few tiny exceptions.

Vital exceptions in terms of marketing direction, focus. And, he had to admit, probable success.

Why couldn't she be just a pretty face and hot body? Her proposal was outstanding. The risk was minimal, the possible benefits innumerable. Damn. Mitch ground his teeth in frustration as the businessman in him overrode the horndog.

"This is a great plan," he reluctantly admitted. "By focusing on the paparazzi-hounded stars, we can provide the perfect getaway for the rich and famous. We'd amp up the security, spread the word that this is a photo-free zone." As ideas started to flow, Mitch grabbed a pen. "Special training for the staff, non-disclosure agreements, legal repercussions."

"Privacy is vital, but it's just one benefit," she cautioned. "Don't lose sight of the bigger picture. Yes, you want to bring in the Hollywood crowd. Once word gets out that you're offering a safe haven from the voracious press, combined with the buzz about how fab your resort is, I guarantee they'll be interested. But that's not going to be enough."

Mitch barely heard her, he was so focused on getting his

flying thoughts on paper. Then Belle slid another folder on top of his notes.

He should have known. She was an event planner, and her initial plan hadn't mentioned a single party or gala. His eyes narrowed as he read the event outline.

"You do want to turn my resort into a sex club," he exclaimed in shock.

"Not exactly," she denied, with a shrug that reminded him that her breasts were less than a foot from his mouth. Luckily her words were enough distraction. Almost.

"I'm suggesting you focus on indulgence of the most decadent kind. Couples' massages, chocolate baths, midnight champagne dinners by the lake. All romantic enough on their own, but you'll offer a few extras. I've got tons of ideas, and I'll share them if we go to contract on this. But basically, you'll have to take your standard resort offering and sex it up. Make it hot and inviting with just a hint of depravity. You do that and I guarantee you'll reel in the jaded Hollywood crowd."

"Depravity? Like what? On-call hookers and pole-dancing lessons?"

"There's nothing depraved about pole-dancing," she chided. "I do it and it's great exercise." She gave him a heavy-lidded look that promised all sorts of pulse-raising benefits. "Someday I'll show you."

Did nothing faze her? Mitch had to laugh.

"The difference between a high-class sex club and a luxury resort offering decadent indulgence is vast, Mitch." Her tone turned serious as all teasing flirtation left her face. "A sex club is cheap, base. It's all about the pickup, the kink, the instant satisfaction. You'd be offering a safe haven for your guests to indulge themselves in all ways, including their sexual fantasies. Masquerade balls, a menu that includes reputed aphrodisiacs, a lingerie shop in the lobby. Pure luxury in perfect keeping with the rest of your resort's offerings. Nothing tacky or low-class."

Decadent indulgence? She was right. That would definitely mesh with the extravagant luxury he'd planned to offer. As far as hooks went, it was certainly fresh. Definitely better than anything his marketing department had come up with.

But it meant focusing his business on sex. And working with Belle. Two things that he'd learned the hard way should never go hand in hand.

Mitch leaned back in his chair, both to show control and because he needed to put some distance between him and Belle's hypnotic scent. He glanced at the Eventfully Yours contract, then gave her an assessing look through narrowed eyes.

"This plan has potential, I'll give you that," he acknowledged. "But I have to ask, what's to keep me from handing you back this contract, unsigned, and running with the plan on my own?"

"Ethics, of course." Belle's look was pure, pitying amusement. "You're one of the good guys, Mitch. You believe in helping others, not screwing them over."

He pulled a face. Yeah, she had him there.

"Besides," she continued as she studied her well-manicured nails, "you can't pull it off without my contacts. At least, not to the level necessary to be the kind of success you're looking for. And then there's the fact that if you do try without me, I'd take the plan to three hotels and resorts within driving distance and offer them the same idea. People are going to try to copy you down the road, but if you lose the exclusivity right out of the gate, you're guaranteed failure."

Damn. So she was hell on wheels as a businesswoman. Mitch knew he should be disgruntled, but he only felt an odd sort of admiring pride.

She read the frustration on his face and laughed. With a wicked look, she leaned forward and patted his cheek.

"Don't worry, you'll love working with me. I'm…fabulous," she purred. The innuendo made Mitch want to whimper.

"You realize if I give you this contract, sex between us is out of the question." He tossed the words out like a drowning man going down for the last time. *At least while they worked together,* he amended in his head. He wasn't stupid or delusional. He knew, sooner or later, they'd be doing the nasty. But he planned on calling the shots, and working together would make it much later than his body wanted.

"If that's the way you want it," she said agreeably. From the wattage of her smile, she was just as happy he'd issued the ultimatum. Damn her.

Mitch frowned, wondering if he'd miscalculated Belle. She came across as hot and sexy. Her nature, her demeanor and vibe were pure sensuality. Was it all an act? A hot front shielding a cold core? A tool to twist a guy by his dick so she could easily lead him around?

"You're fine with that," he clarified.

"Of course," she said, sliding off his desk. With a quick twitch of her hand, she straightened her skirt and made sure her blouse was tucked into the wide leather belt circling her tiny waist. He clenched his teeth to keep from drooling as she bent over to pick up her bag, and wished like hell he'd refused outright to work with her.

He forced his gaze from her ass to the folder, contents and plans spread over his desk blotter. No, he couldn't regret considering her for the job. Her take on the resort's events and focus was the most dynamic he'd ever seen.

He could wish they'd done the dirty on the desk first, though. Mitch stifled a sigh and came around to the front of his desk to escort her out.

Belle turned to give him a wide smile and held out her hand. Seal the deal with a handshake, he supposed.

When he took her delicate palm in his, she dropped their hands so, enfolded, they rested on her hip. Then she closed the distance between them until her breasts were a hair's-breadth away from his chest. Mitch's erection returned, granite-hard.

Her gaze locked on his, Belle leaned forward. Up on her tiptoes, she used her breasts against his chest for balance. She wrapped one hand around the back of his neck and gave a gentle tug, pulling his mouth down to meet hers.

Both fascinated and turned on, Mitch let her take the lead. She was the most sexually confident women he'd ever met. Yet beneath it all, he sensed the same sweet vulnerability that had hooked him six years before. The sweetness, he knew, would be his downfall if he wasn't careful.

Not willing to show her how strong her power was, he held himself still as her lips pressed, soft and lush, against his. His hands itched to pull her close, to press her tight against his body so he could feel her curves surrendering.

Then her tongue, so soft and seductive, traced the line of his mouth. A quick flick to the corners, a soft slide across his lower lip. Blood roared through Mitch's head, drowning out all caution. When her teeth nipped, just a little, at his lip, he lost it.

His hands dove into her hair, holding her head still as his tongue took hers in a wild dance of pleasure. Slip, slide, intense and delicious, he gave way to the power of their kiss.

More, was all he could think. He had to have more.

He didn't know if it was that desperately needy thought or the sound of his groan that pulled him back to sanity. Unable to do otherwise, knowing it would likely be his last chance to taste her for God knew how long, Mitch slowly ended the kiss.

With a moan of approval, Belle stepped away. Her eyes, blurry with desire, stared into his as she ran her tongue over her bottom lip and gave a sigh. Then her mouth curved in a smile that screamed satisfaction.

"You'll give me the contract," she assured him, her words a husky promise. "And we'll have incredible sex. And in the end, you'll be thanking your lucky stars you were smart enough to do both."

3

"I BLEW IT," Belle insisted, pacing her office. The plush carpet warmed her bare feet as she stomped from one end of the room to the other. "I got so caught up in the sexual game, in wanting to show Mitch what he'd lost by wanting some business deal more than me, I lost sight of why I was there."

"Chill," Sierra said, ensconced behind Belle's desk while working on a seating plan. "You haven't blown it. Mitch is a by-the-book kind of guy. When he's ready to reject both of your propositions he'll have his assistant e-mail you."

Despite her anxiety, Belle snorted and gave a rueful shake of her head. No patty-cake from Sierra, nope. The brunette shot from the hip, to hell with the fatalities.

"You think he'll have his tidy little assistant send me a no-thanks-on-the-sex e-mail?"

"Nah," Sierra said as she frowned at the sketch, then checked her guest list. "He'll make it all businesslike. You know, something like, 'I appreciate your time and creative proposal, but have decided it doesn't suit my needs. As clever and inventive as your suggestions are, I don't feel that's the right direction to take at this time. Oh, by the way, I'm not hiring you for the event gig, either.'"

The rejection sounded so realistic, Belle almost rushed to her laptop to see if Sierra was reading it verbatim.

"Did you hear something?" she asked suspiciously.

Sierra just rolled her eyes.

"We've been friends since training bras and boarding school, and in all these years, I've never seen you turn stupid over any guy but this one," Sierra pointed out. "Maybe we'd be better off if he does turn the deal down. I don't think he's good for you."

"He tasted good," Belle muttered. Tasted good, felt good, looked good. Her breath shuddered as she remembered how amazing his kiss had been. She'd only intended to prove a point, tease him a little. He'd been the one with the point, though. Hard and long, pressing into her thigh.

God, she was going crazy with wanting him.

"You're doing it again," Sierra reminded.

Belle glanced over at her friend, surprised to see she'd pushed aside her seating chart and was unwrapping a butterscotch candy. Sierra only resorted to sugar, and only in tiny amounts, when she was really stressed. Given the half-dozen unwrapped pieces in front of her, she was definitely worried.

"Doing what again?" Belle asked.

"Getting stupid," Sierra repeated. "It's like an automatic shutoff button gets flipped whenever you get near Mitch Carter. Your brain goes into hibernate mode."

Belle rolled her eyes and dropped into the chair opposite Sierra. "Don't be silly. I'm just hot for the guy. You've seen him, he's gorgeous. Sexy, smart and fun. That doesn't make me stupid, that makes me horny."

"I've seen you horny before. You don't blow business deals over horny," Sierra said, chomping down on the candy with a loud crunch.

Belle winced at the sound. That had to hurt the teeth. Then her eyes went round as Sierra unwrapped another and popped it into her mouth.

Best friends since they were fourteen, the two women knew

each other inside out. Belle had never considered anyone else to go into business with. Guilt trickled down her spine. And now she was stressing her friend into a sugar coma.

"I didn't blow it," Belle defended. At least, she didn't think she did. "I might have gotten a bit carried away, but a little flirting won't affect the deal. He loved my spiel. He was impressed with our ideas. Whether we get it or we don't will depend on whether he's open to the sexual angle or not. For the resort," she quickly added.

Sierra chewed up another hard candy without replying. She gave Belle a long, considering look, then unwrapped another piece.

The look was a familiar one. She'd worn it when she'd talked Belle into taking a chance on their business. She wore it when she told a client their request was over-the-top crazy. She always wore it when she told Belle her outfit sucked or her ideas were lame. It was her truth-at-all-costs look.

Belle hated that look.

For the good of her own ears and Sierra's dental bill, Belle reached over and scooped up the remaining candy.

"Belle, you barely knew this guy and you were willing to toss aside your principles and beliefs. For what? A piece of ass."

"I'm not some dumb tramp," Belle snapped back. "I might have been distracted during that meeting, but I'll be damned if I gave away a single principle and I sure as hell didn't ignore my beliefs."

Whatever that was supposed to mean, she fumed. God, if she didn't hate confrontation so much, she'd yell at her friend. Tell her to quit being so negative, so mistrusting. Instead she sucked in a deep, calming breath and reminded herself that this was just Sierra's way.

"I meant six years ago, when you agreed to marry the guy just so you could get in his pants," Sierra corrected with a roll of her eyes. "You weren't interested in happy-ever-after back then. But you gave in despite your better judgment. And look how that turned out."

Belle winced. She'd rather not think about it. "Please, do you think Mitch would be crazy enough to propose to me again? All he wanted was a leg up the ladder, and he doesn't need that any longer."

"You don't say anything about whether you'd be crazy enough to accept a proposal," Sierra pointed out.

"I didn't think I had to state the obvious. I gave up believing in fairy tales or happy-ever-after. I'm hot for the guy, okay? That's it. I know better than to risk anything other than a little time and some sexy lingerie."

"I hope so. I really, really hope so," Sierra said, her words dripping with doubt. "Because your history says otherwise."

A chime snagged her attention and Sierra glanced at the laptop. She clicked the mouse a couple times and heaved a sigh. Belle's stomach dropped to her toes at the look on her partner's face.

"Okay, here's the deal," the sleek brunette said in her no-nonsense tone. "If we get this contract, I need you to make me a promise."

Belle eyed the computer, her fingers itching to grab it and see what message had prompted Sierra's ultimatum.

"What's the promise?" Belle hedged. She wasn't about to agree to anything crazy, like keeping her hands off Mitch. Yes, she might lose a few brain cells around him. But she was an intelligent woman, she had extras.

Replaying those excuses through her head, Belle heaved a sigh and privately admitted they were bullshit. This job was huge, and not only to Eventfully Yours. If she pulled it off, made friendly—but not *that* friendly—with Mitch, there was a good chance he'd help her dad.

Belle thought back to the call she'd had that morning from her father's secretary. Her dad was stressed again, and even though he was supposed to be home recovering from his heart attack, he'd spent the last four days running to the office trying to find some way out of the mess he was in. Between a series of bad investments, the real-estate crash and a sucky economy, Forsham Hotels was sinking fast. A wave of helpless frustration washed over her. She had to do something, anything, to get Mitch to talk to her dad.

Maybe Twisted Knickers lingerie carried chastity belts.

Sierra took a deep breath. Belle was nodding before her friend could even issue the request. Fine, no sex.

"As soon as you can, hell, the first day if possible, you haul Mitch Carter into the nearest closet and have wild monkey sex with him," Sierra commanded. "Have as much sex as possible. Do it as many times in as many ways as you can. Get it all out of your system. Do it on the ceiling if you have to. Use toys and kinky leather getups."

Belle's jaw dropped. She shook her head, sure her hearing was faulty.

"For the good of Eventfully Yours, for the good of your thought processes and, most of all, for the good of my sanity, I'm begging you—" Sierra placed both palms on the desk and leaned forward, her face intense "—do him. Immediately."

It took all Belle's strength to lift her chin off her chest. Sierra was a dyed-in-the-wool cynic, but she'd never been this…well, pragmatic about deliberately seducing someone.

Belle kind of liked it. Even if it was insane.

"You're kidding, right? I thought you were worried about my poor judgment with Mitch?"

"I'm worried about your judgment when your head is clouded with unrequited lust," Sierra shot back. "Once you've screwed his brains out a few times you'll be fine."

"Fine?"

"I've read studies that list all the ways sexual frustration hinders a person. This exact situation wasn't on the list, but I'm sure it qualifies. Once the sexual curiosity is sated, you'll be your normal, savvy self and kick butt with this deal."

"So this is for the good of our business?" Belle's tummy did a wicked somersault.

Shouldn't she feel excited instead of nervous? Sierra was the voice of reason, so her encouragement made the whole idea seem…well, weird.

"Sure," Sierra returned with a shrug.

"We got the deal?" Belle pointed to the computer and whatever message Sierra was hiding.

"We've got a shot at the deal. He wants a meeting to discuss it." She spun the laptop around so Belle could read the message from Mitch's assistant. Lunch meeting, tomorrow afternoon. Come prepared to negotiate.

Excitement buzzed through Belle's system like electricity. Her stomach tumbled, nerves and anticipation warning her to eat ahead of time. Yes. This was her chance, her shot at everything she wanted. She'd show him the fine art of negotiation…her way.

Belle gave a wicked laugh of delight. "Never let it be said I'm not willing to give my all for the cause."

While she didn't quite share Sierra's anxiety that she'd blow the deal or do something stupid, she wasn't about to turn down a direct order to hunt down the hottest guy she'd ever lusted after and screw his brains out.

As a WAITER topped off his coffee, Mitch patted the pocket where he'd tucked the faded cocktail napkin with its gold foil inscription of his and Belle's names and their former wedding date. He'd spent two days dissecting Eventfully Yours's proposal with his management team, listening to their analysis and opinions. The unanimous belief was that of all the proposals, this was unquestionably the strongest. The best. And in Mitch's opinion, the biggest pain in the ass.

Not because the plan would be difficult to implement. All that meant was he had to work harder, smarter, than the average guy. Since he'd built his reputation doing just that, he never shied from difficult.

Proof positive was right here, he thought as he looked around Spago Restaurant. Airy, bright and lush, it was one of the top restaurants in L.A. He'd have had to save up for a month just to bring Belle to have a drink here when they were engaged. But not anymore. Six years and a driving need to prove himself to her, to everyone—including his former father-in-law-to-be—who'd thought he'd marry his way to success, had given him a much stronger edge.

So no, he didn't blink at taking on the difficult. But this plan came with his personal version of kryptonite: Belle Forsham. The one woman guaranteed not only to bring him to his knees, but to make sure he loved the hell out of being there.

Working with her could be a disaster. If he let himself get off track, the results would be ugly. He had everything on the line here. Not only the resort, but his investors' money and trust. To say nothing of his reputation. Sex with Belle wasn't worth risking all that. Which was why he was only agreeing to part of her proposal. The events, specifically.

As intriguing, and probably lucrative, as the sex themes had been, he didn't trust himself to deal with her on that level. She was simply too much temptation. He was afraid she'd use those themes to take that hot kiss one or two—or twenty—steps farther.

So—he fingered the napkin again—he'd keep her at arm's length. Business, pure and simple. Hell, he'd been burned once, he was a smart man. He knew how to keep his fingers—and other body parts—to himself. If he was otherwise tempted, he had his talisman as a reminder that Belle was off-limits.

Suddenly, as though someone had pushed a button, his body went on full alert. His senses flared as he glanced across the restaurant, not surprised to see Belle making her way toward him. Sleek and sexy in a simple spring dress of the palest pink, she sauntered between the linen-covered tables, her eyes never leaving his. Standing as she approached, Mitch eyed her half smile, the hint of naughty amusement igniting his body to instant lust.

His body would just have to get over it.

"Thanks for meeting me," he said as he gestured to the chair the waiter held out. "I'm sure you have a busy schedule."

Her green eyes narrowed as if she were trying to read his tone, then Belle gave a little shrug and murmured her thanks to the waiter.

"My schedule's never too busy for you," she returned, spreading the napkin over her lap without releasing his gaze. "Unless, of course, you're planning a wedding or something. Then I might have to run."

Mitch's jaw sagged. The mischievous humor gleaming in her eyes assured him he hadn't heard wrong. Leave it to Belle to poke fun at something taboo. It wasn't just her smile that was naughty.

"I don't think you'll need your sneakers anytime soon," he deadpanned. "My tux is at the cleaners."

Her laugh rang out, garnering a few indulgent smiles from other diners and sparking an irritatingly warm feeling in Mitch's belly.

"Whew. Good thing, since I don't even own a pair. Let's have lunch and talk business, instead. Okay?"

On cue, the waiter stepped over and handed Belle a menu. She barely glanced at it before ordering iced tea and salad. Interesting. Either she dined at four-star restaurants often enough to be blasé about the famous menu or she really was focused on business. Mitch wondered if she'd been here before, and what kind of men she dated. Irritated at his train of thought, he shoved aside the jealous curiosity and gave the waiter his order. The only thing he needed to know about her activities of the past six years was in reference to her business.

"Your assistant said you had questions, wanted to discuss Eventfully Yours's proposal in more depth?" she said, her tone professional. Her look, though, was pure sex. Glossy lips pursed, she let her gaze do a slow, appreciative slide over his face and chest. Mitch was grateful the table was between them, both preventing her from going any further and keeping his reaction hidden.

She arched a brow in query. The gleam in her eyes told him she knew she was sending mixed signals and was looking forward to seeing which ones he chose to pick up.

"I do have questions," Mitch said, his tone neutral. He wasn't going to play her game, but damned if he'd let her know that. Keeping her guessing was his only shot at maintaining the upper hand. And with Belle, he needed all the control he could get. She was like a wily dominatrix, luring him in with sugar and spice but hiding a whip and chain behind her back.

With that in mind, he pulled out his file of questions, suggestions and ideas. Through the rest of the meal he and Belle hammered out details for the grand opening, as well as a series of smaller pre-events that would build buzz for the resort. He was again impressed with her savvy suggestions, especially as she expanded on her proposal, filling in the crucial details that she'd held back initially.

Damn, she was good.

By dessert, she'd gone from good to mind-blowing.

"You're going to want to redesign the landscaping here and here," she said, poking at the sketch of the resort's property with one blunt fingernail. "If you bring in some fully mature trees, a few more bushes, you'll have a perfect sex-in-the-woods setting. Guests will love that, and if you set it up right they'll think it's their little secret."

Definitely mind-blowing. And thanks to comments like that, all he could think of were other things he'd like her to blow.

"You've obviously considered everything," he said. He wondered if keeping him in a constant state of arousal was planned as well. Glancing at the amused awareness in her eyes, he figured it was. "Now about your suggested themes…"

"I noticed you kept changing the subject when I brought them up." There was no judgment in her eyes, only curiosity. "So, what? You're going to go vanilla?"

"Vanilla?"

"Safe and tame."

Ahh, there was the irritation. Mitch grinned in relief.

"Let's just say I don't think the two of us focusing on sex is a good idea," he returned.

"Chicken?"

"Prudent."

Belle rolled her eyes. "Safe sex again?"

He couldn't deny it. After all, the safest sex was abstinence.

"Because of our past association I think we should discuss our history and clear the air," he said instead. "I want us both to be on solid ground, which means we need to deal with any past resentments or issues."

For the first time in memory, Mitch watched Belle's expressive face close up. Like a door slamming, it simply went blank and unwelcoming. Then, so fast he wondered if he'd imagined it, she gave a roll of her eyes and flashed her sassy smile.

"The past is over, Mitch. I promise, I'm not bringing any old baggage to the table." She leaned forward, and for the first time since she'd waltzed out of his office two days earlier, touched him. A whisper-soft brush of her fingertips over the back of his hand. Gentle, teasing, easy. Heat flared, instant and hot, in his belly. "Any desire I have to chase you around is definitely fresh and new, not a leftover itch."

"You don't own sneakers, remember?" he snapped, equal parts irritated that she'd so easily closed the door to their past before he could find out why she'd really run off and relieved not to have to admit to his own part in their failed history. "So we'll just keep chasing off our list of things to do."

"Then what's the problem?"

"Like I said, given our history, I think it's wise to keep the sexual temptation to a minimum." He'd rehearsed and rehashed his next words multiple times since he'd decided to work with her, but Mitch still had trouble voicing them. "I've also written up the contracts event by event, rather than the job as a whole."

"Care to clarify that?" He'd had no idea her husky voice could turn to ice.

"I have everything riding on the success of this resort. That success will depend greatly on how well the events are handled. I have to depend on these events happening. As amazing as your proposal is, I can't afford to tie myself up for more than one event at a time given the circumstances of our last…association."

If he'd reached across the table and slapped her, she couldn't have looked more shocked. Mitch felt like a first-class bastard. Belle's luscious mouth parted as if to challenge him, her eyes sparkling with fury. Then, as if a switch had flipped, she sucked in her bottom lip and gave a jerky little shrug.

"No way. I'm sorry, but these mini-events are back to back, each one leading up to the grand opening. Eventfully Yours won't take the job without at least the pre- and grand opening events contracted." Her tone was pure business, her eyes shuttered.

The fairness of her words, spoken in that even, businesslike tone, made Mitch realize he was the one letting the past get in the way.

"That's fine," he agreed. "We'll contract for the five smaller events and the grand opening."

"Great. Unless there are any more grudges you're harboring, I'd say we're good to go."

"No grudges." At least, none he'd admit. "Like I said, just being prudent."

She rolled her eyes again, but the gesture didn't hide the hurt lurking in the sea-green depths. Mitch frowned, irritated that the sight made him feel like a jerk.

"Then we have a deal," she said, her tone making it clear she was glad to close the history book. Mitch was surprised, since most women were only too happy to discuss the past in all its gory details. "I'll be at the resort a week from Monday. Given the distance from L.A. and how much work is involved, I'll require a room on-site, of course. A suite would be best as I'll set up office there."

Belle opened a file, made and initialed a few adjustments on the contract to reflect his changes. With a flourish, she signed her name, then slid the papers back in the folder.

She handed it to him with a wink. Apparently she'd regained her good humor.

"I think I'll put you in one of the cottages," he returned. "Unlike the suites, they're already furnished and should suit you perfectly."

"How far are these cottages from your on-site office?"

"You can call me anytime you have questions," he assured her. And the distance would make him think twice about dropping in to visit.

Her brow creased, her eyes rounded. "You're starting to make me think you're harboring more issues, Mitch. Are you planning to avoid me the entire time I'm working with you?"

Not Belle, per se. Just sex with her. Mitch winced. There was no way he wouldn't sound like a pompous ass, but he had to make things clear.

"Please don't take this the wrong way, Belle. But I'm not going to sleep with you. We're doing business together, and business and pleasure just don't mix."

"Hmm, interesting. Too bad you didn't think that six years ago when you tried to mix your business with my daddy's and in the process ruined my pleasure."

He frowned, but before he could respond, she gave a quick shake of her head and a brittle, dismissive little laugh. "Now that does sound like I'm the one harboring some of those issues you're worried about. Let's start fresh, okay? I'm not the same person I was before and I'm betting you aren't, either."

He opened his mouth to retort, but closed it again. All of a sudden, he wanted to clear the air, to ask her the reasons behind her bridal dash. But to do so meant acknowledging emotions he'd locked away. Admitting mistakes he regretted. And worse, bridging the chasm of mistrust that the past kept firmly between them. As long as it was there, he knew they'd never have a shot at intimacy.

He slid his hand into his pocket and fingered the wedding napkin. Between his talisman and that chasm, he'd be safe from screwing up. He couldn't afford to lose again.

"I've changed a lot in six years," was all he said.

"So have I," she assured him as she laid one warm, smooth hand over his. Energy, mostly sexual but with a subtle layer of something else Mitch couldn't define, shot through his body at her touch. The most platonic connection, and he was hard, hot and horny. It boggled the mind to think what his response would be if they had full body contact. Chasm and talisman, he reminded himself.

"I hope you're not upset," he said, telling himself it was guilt and not lust making him want to pull her onto his lap. "You're a gorgeous, sexy woman. You don't need to be chasing a guy."

"Who said I'd chase you?" she asked, her tone light and amused.

Mitch frowned. He knew he hadn't misunderstood her signal or her flirting words.

"Like you, I'm much smarter than I was six years ago. Smart enough to know better than to chase a man. Especially a man like you."

Mitch opened his mouth to deny that she'd chased him before, but she continued before he could get a single word out. "You say we won't have sex. I say we will. Simple difference of opinion and only time will tell which one of us is right. And if you're too uptight to do two things at once successfully, that's fine. I can wait."

"What the hell are you talking about?" he asked, watching nonplussed as she slid her folder into her briefcase and got to her feet. "What two things?"

"Rock your resort opening and have wild monkey sex with me," she shot back as she turned to leave. "When it happens, I won't have chased you to get it. You'll be the one doing the chasing…and the begging."

4

BELLE GLANCED over the guest list for the pre-opening event and added two more names. Actors, politicians, celebutants. She needed to scatter in some high-profile musicians, but she wanted to do a little more research first.

Almost two weeks had passed since her lunch with Mitch and she'd yet to spend any time alone with him. The first week was understandable. She'd been working from her office in L.A., finalizing things and tying up loose ends so she could spend the next few weeks here at Lakeside. The resort was a hundred miles from her office, and it was only practical that she work on-site for the duration. She'd figured the bonus would be seeing Mitch day in and day out for the next three weeks. Not only would she relish the sexual thrill, but she could drop a few hints and feel him out on the topic of her father.

But since she'd arrived to find her cozy cottage ready and waiting, he'd been avoiding her. And he wasn't even trying to hide the fact.

The perfect host, he'd had fresh flowers waiting in her room. But he'd sent his assistant to help her settle in. He'd remembered her preferences, making sure she had hot tea and a basket of muffins delivered each morning, but he'd avoided seeing her unless there were at least three other people in the room.

Today she was supposed to tour the grounds, the suites and

the spa. And knowing Mitch, he'd send his rabbity assistant to do the honors.

She thought of her promise to Sierra. Do him. Fast, furious, as soon as possible. So far, she was failing dismally. Sexual frustration was never comfortable, but she was a big girl and could handle losing the game. But Mitch hadn't even manned-up enough to play. She recalled his declaration that sex between them was off-limits. This must be his way of making sure she knew he was serious.

Well, so was she. And seduction wasn't going to work. It hadn't when they'd been engaged, it hadn't when they'd met again a couple of weeks ago. She obviously needed a new plan.

Nibbling on her second blueberry muffin, she punched a button on her cell phone, leaving it on speaker.

"Morning," Sierra answered cheerfully. "I take it you haven't died of sexual frustration yet?"

"I'm surviving," Belle said dryly. "Barely, though. I need your help."

"Sorry, sweets. You're not my type."

"Ha-ha. I need ideas, you dork. Mitch is running scared. He's avoiding me except for e-mails and the telephone. Try as I might I can't even get him to have phone sex with me."

"Shit," Sierra muttered. Belle heard the clink of glass against glass and knew her friend was topping off her coffee. Sierra always thought best when highly caffeinated.

"I need a plan," Belle said, stating the obvious.

"No kidding. Otherwise I'll be shopping for some ugly bridesmaid's dress again."

"Hey, the dress wasn't that ugly."

"Anything in Easter-egg pink is ugly and that's beside the point." Belle could hear the tap-tap-tapping of Sierra's nails against the coffee cup. "Give me a rundown of what you've done on the job while I think."

Belle thought best while lounging in a bubble bath or lazing in the sun, something that allowed her to relax and let the ideas flow. Sierra, though, was the opposite, needing noise and activity to find her solutions.

Pulling her notebook toward her, Belle went over the timeline and to-do list. On the off chance she managed to convince Mitch to consider the theme idea, she'd ordered sex-toy samples, sketched out three separate theme ideas and started the plans for the pre-opening event. To garner word-of-mouth buzz and set the tone for privacy, she'd suggested that Mitch hold a low-key non-advertised event before the media caught wind of the resort's offerings. It would offer that semblance of privacy while giving their potential guests a taste of just how special a stay at Lakeside would be.

"Quit flirting," Sierra said, interrupting Belle's recitation of the tentative guest list.

"I was reading in my most serious tone," Belle responded with a sniff. "I can't help it if my voice excites you."

"Ha. Seriously though, your last encounter with Mitch, you tossed down the gauntlet. I don't blame you, of course, but still, the guy is definitely running scared."

Belle wrinkled her nose and pushed away what was left of her muffin. The idea of Mitch wanting nothing to do with her ruined her appetite.

"I told him I wouldn't chase him and I'm not," she defended, her tone stiff. "But is it asking too much that he meet with me without the chaperones?"

"You need to change tactics, lull him into complacency then reel him in."

"Lull him from afar?" Her pouty tone was only half-pretend.

"He's going to have to meet with you sooner or later," Sierra assured her. "Once he does, turn the tables. Play the professional card. You know, pretend you're there to work, to do a job."

This time Belle really did pout. "I *am* here to do a job."

"Yeah, yeah. But we both know you have ulterior motives. He's not stupid, so he probably suspects it, too. So confuse him."

"Professional?"

"More focus on the job, the reasons you're there. Including needing Mitch's help for your dad." Glass clinked as Sierra got even more coffee. "Less focus on how cute his ass is."

What, was she blind? Belle wanted to argue, but knew there was no point. Too much was at stake. Not only the job itself, but Eventfully Yours's reputation and her father's business. Mitch had made his disinterest plenty clear; she'd respect his decision.

"Have you talked to him any more about the theme program?" Sierra asked, obviously taking Belle's silence as agreement to her plan.

"I haven't seen him to pitch it any further," Belle reminded her.

Silence.

Belle sighed. "I'll send him an e-mail. He seems to like those."

She and Sierra wrapped up a few more details then hung up, leaving Belle to feel like a total slacker. Sierra was right. She'd been so focused on her attraction to Mitch, she'd let her priorities slip. Well, no more. She grabbed her pen and started a list of what she needed to do to set things right.

Before she could write more than a few things, though, her cell phone chimed the "Boogie-Woogie Blues."

"Daddy," she greeted in answer. "How are you feeling?"

"I'm feeling sick and tired of being asked that question, princess," Franklin Forsham growled.

"People ask because they care, not out of some twisted desire to be irritating. You need to rest and give yourself time to recuperate. Quadruple bypass is nothing to blow off."

"I'm sitting on my ass instead of golfing, aren't I? That's

recuperation enough." The pain of that was clear in his voice. Frank Forsham loved nothing more than a good game of golf. Belle glanced out the window at the gorgeous tree-studded view. Off in the distance the sun glinted, jewel-like, off the lake, and beyond that was what Diana had claimed to be a first-class golf course. Not big enough to bring in the major tournaments, but challenging enough to keep the guests entertained.

Her father would love it. Maybe after she got him and Mitch together, he'd come play a few rounds. She didn't consider it naive to believe it would happen any more than she considered herself overoptimistic to think she and Mitch would get together. Faith and hard work. She figured as long as she had both—and some hot lingerie—she was set.

"Of course, I wouldn't be able to golf anyway, given the state of things here," he grumbled, stealing her attention back from her idyllic imaginings. "Damned market is only getting worse. Forsham Hotels hasn't been hit this hard since the early seventies."

Belle listened to her father's description of the state of his company. She knew enough about business to realize he was actually making light of how bad it was. Worse, though, was the tension she heard in his voice. He was supposed to be recovering, not working himself into another heart attack.

"It'll turn around and everything will be fine, Daddy," she said, even though they both knew it was an empty promise. But as always, Franklin didn't expect any real input or contribution from her, so he let the comment go unchallenged. She was his pretty little girl, no more, no less. Belle had long ago given up the idea of proving herself to him. But maybe, just maybe, he'd respect her a little if she saved his company?

"Come by tonight, we'll go to dinner," he ordered.

Belle glanced at her to-do list. Even if she rescheduled the tour, her plate was full. Added to that, it would take her an hour and a half to drive back to L.A., longer if she hit traffic. She flipped the page in her planner, noting an early breakfast meeting with the spa manager.

Then she thought of her dad, alone in that big rambling house.

"I'll be there at seven," she promised. "I wanted to talk to you, anyway."

"About?"

"Um, I sort of ran into someone from the past and thought you'd like to hear about him."

"Him?"

She hated it when he did that. Single-word questions, then silence that made her feel as if she had to spill tons of details to fill the empty space.

"Mitch Carter," she said. Then she cringed and waited.

But not for long.

"That cheating sonofabitch? I thought he'd run back to the east coast where he belongs."

Belle winced. "Dad, I told you, Mitch didn't cheat."

"Harrumph."

"He didn't. Really. He just sort of misled me. I'm sure he thinks I did much worse, leaving him at the altar like that."

"He was a lucky man and he blew it."

Belle pressed her lips together. She had to get her dad to quit hating Mitch or there was no point in pushing Mitch to help him. Leave it to her to be stuck between two stubborn men.

"Let's talk about it over dinner, okay?"

"Let's not. I don't want to discuss the cheater or that debacle that was your wedding. Especially not when it's thanks to him that I invested in that damned property. His connections and contracting license were supposed to get us past the stupid zoning regulations. Thanks to his duplicity, I'm stuck. Can't build, can't sell."

Her father continued to mutter. Belle's stomach twisted.

She'd told her father the day after the wedding that Mitch hadn't been with any other women, that she hadn't meant to imply anything like that. But her father had blown up at her, ranting about the humiliation and misplaced trust. Too horrified to ask if he meant his trust in Mitch or his trust in her, she'd gulped down her explanation and run from the room.

Her father's attitude didn't bode well for her little save-Forsham-Hotels plan. But she'd worry about convincing him later. For now, she needed to focus on getting Mitch to listen to her. That was enough of a challenge.

With that in mind, she bade her father an absent-minded goodbye, promising to see him that evening. As soon as she hung up, she grabbed the cottage phone and dialed star-seven.

"Diana? Hey, I need to postpone the tour until tomorrow, okay?"

"Is there a problem?" Mitch's assistant asked in her hesitant tone.

"Not at all. I just have to run home for the evening. An offer came up that I couldn't refuse."

"Business?"

"No, dinner…" With her father? No, just in case Diana shared the excuse with Mitch, she didn't want to bring her father into the mix until she'd had time to butter them both up. "A dinner date."

"WHAT IN THE HELL do you mean, the program crashed?"

The hotel manager winced, then he gave a helpless shrug. Tall, skinny and blond, Larry looked like a morose scarecrow. Mitch had hand-picked him to run the resort because he handled the staff like a gifted choreographer and knew hotels inside out. And, theoretically, hotel computers. "We don't understand what happened. I've spent the morning on the phone with tech support—they're baffled, too."

The computerized reservation program was supposed to be bug-free, idiot-proof and have both on- and off-site backups. "You recovered the lost data, right?"

"We're working on it. The system has a backup, but somehow, well, the battery went dead."

Mitch closed his eyes and shook his head. Continual construction delays. The pipes had burst in the pool room, there was a gopher infestation on the golf course, and now this? Seriously, who had his voodoo doll and why the hell were they jabbing it so hard?

The only person he'd recently pissed off was Belle. And he couldn't see her going the voodoo route. She was too direct for that. She'd rather see him on his knees begging. Or maybe just on his knees.

"Get it fixed," he instructed tiredly. As soon as the manager left, Mitch lifted his phone and punched a button.

"Do you believe jobs can be cursed?" he asked as soon as Reece answered.

"Nah, that's the kind of thing suits like you come up with as an excuse for falling on their ass."

"Well, my ass is definitely getting bruised," Mitch acknowledged. "I'm starting to think it's more than a learning curve."

"You don't really believe that curse crap, do you? You want me to fly you out a witch doctor?"

"If I thought it'd make a difference, I'd have you hand-deliver one."

Reece laughed, although Mitch was only half joking. "Gotta hand it to you, cuz, you're the most hands-on guy I know. Guess that's why you're kicking butt. You stick your fingers in every pie you deal in, swinging a hammer as easily as you make those slick deals."

Not quite *every* pie. Mitch had been doing his damnedest to avoid the sweetie pie that was his ex. Not trusting himself around her, he'd justified his absence by putting Diana in charge of the events projects. And Belle was the Party Princess, after all. She didn't need his supervision to plan a successful event.

"Seriously, what's the deal?" Reece, or Cowboy, as Mitch's cousin and security guru was aptly nicknamed, sounded as concerned as he ever did. Which meant his drawl had slowed and the teasing humor had left his voice.

Mitch listed the resort's problems-du-jour, from construction to rodent infestation to computer crash. He was explaining about the staff issues when his cousin interrupted.

"Your event gal quit? Just like that? The hot little redhead who loved to party? What happened?"

"She's in rehab."

"No shit? What're you going to do about that opening weekend party you were so hot to have?"

"If I can't stop this streak of bad luck, there won't be an opening," Mitch hedged, not wanting to mention Belle's involvement in the resort. Since Reece had been his best man, he had a pretty vivid memory of her. "I'm willing to accept a few problems here and there, but not this level of misfortune."

"Sabotage?"

"That sounds so paranoid."

"It ain't paranoia if they're out to get you," Reece pointed out.

"Right."

The two men were silent for a minute, then Mitch heard Reece shuffling some papers. That his bronc-riding cousin was working in an office amused Mitch. A go-getter Kentucky cowboy, Reece was more suited to riding horseback than riding a desk. Rather than putting his military time to use in law enforcement, he'd opened his own security firm.

"Did you get the note I sent you about new requirements for the resort?" Mitch asked.

"Something about catering to the fancy-ass folks there in Hollywood?"

"That's it. Why don't you send a guy out early? He can start assessing for the upgrades, and poke around a little at the same time."

"Two birds with one stone. Good plan."

They nailed down the details, then hung up. Mitch let his head fall back on the chair, his eyes, as always, going to the view.

Ever since he was a kid, he'd dreamed of a place like this. Oh, not the rich and fancy angle, but of owning something huge, something major. He'd wanted to make his mark, to be special. An only child, he'd been one of seventeen cousins. The last words his dad had spoken to him before he'd died were to tell him to be the man, to take care of his mom and show the world what he was made of. Even at five, Mitch had taken those words to heart.

They'd sparked his desperate need to prove himself. To be important.

Starting out in construction as a teen, he'd worked his way up the ranks in his stepdad's company by the time he'd entered college. He'd graduated with a degree in business and been left the construction firm when his mom and stepdad had died just before his twenty-third birthday. Like Reece said, he'd worked every aspect of his business, from swinging the hammer to marketing property to making deals. Within five years he'd launched his development company and figured he was well on his way to the big time.

But he'd wanted more. Enter Forsham Hotels and the biggest mistake of his life.

Which reminded him…

Mitch pushed away from his desk and strode into Diana's office. As soon as she saw him, the mousy brunette held out a sheaf of papers.

"Larry sent these up," she said.

"Obviously his team hasn't figured out the problem yet," he observed, flipping through the pages of techno-speak as if he had a clue what they said. With a shrug, he tossed the report back on Diana's desk and asked, "Did Belle have a list of suggestions after her tour?"

"Um, not yet." Diana busied herself with shuffling the tech report, then clipping the pages just so.

"She's writing it up?"

"No, I don't think she is."

Mitch's earlier irritation, still bubbling away just below the surface, threatened to erupt.

"I suppose there's a good reason why she hasn't done what I specifically asked?"

"Well, maybe because she had to cancel," his assistant mumbled, bending low to put the tech report in the bottom filing-cabinet drawer.

"Why the hell did she cancel the tour?"

"She had a, well, a date," Diana said, her face almost buried in her keyboard.

Either she'd figured out how irritated he got when people wasted his time on the job or she was still afraid to look him in the face when she gave him bad news. Either way, her timidity pissed him off even more.

"Get her on the phone," he snapped. When Diana winced, Mitch sighed, feeling like he'd kicked a puppy. "Please."

"She's already left the resort. She said since she had to drive into L.A. anyway, she'd leave early and go into town to meet some vendors, store owners and suppliers to look into possible liaisons for the resort."

If Diana's face got any closer to the keyboard, she'd smash her nose on the *H* key. Mitch swallowed a growl and tried to remember all the organizational qualities that made her a great assistant. Maybe he'd better take to carrying a list in his pocket?

"Get her on her cell, then," he barked, this time not bothering to temper his tone. Diana was just going to have to get over her fear, because he didn't have time to baby her. And damned if he hadn't been right about Belle being a flake. Less than a week here at the resort and she was already slacking off.

Date. Fury bolted through him like lightning. Fast, furious, deadly. It was because she was screwing off, he assured himself. Not because she might be screwing some guy other than him.

Reece was right. Mitch had built his success by taking part in every aspect of his business. Every single thing. Which obviously needed to include his luscious ex-fiancée. This hands-off approach wasn't working. Not for the resort, and definitely not for his resort's event planner.

"Her phone goes direct to voice mail," Diana said, dread clear in her tone.

Images of Belle and some faceless guy sent that bolt of fury right through him again, ripping a hole in Mitch's gut.

"I'll deal with Ms. Forsham and the tour tomorrow," he decided. "No more of this letting her do things her way. I'm stepping in and showing her who's boss. From now on, she'll answer to me."

5

HUMMING her favorite pop star's latest song, Belle strode through the resort lobby with a swing in her hips and a smile on her lips. Her heels tapped a pleasing counter-beat as she crossed the polished marble and breathed in the rich scent of fresh flowers from the atrium.

Gorgeous morning. It was weird how good she felt waking up in the enchanted forest, as she'd taken to calling the wooded view outside her bedroom window. Throw in tea and muffins on the tiny, private deck, and she'd managed to shove aside all her worries about her father and grab a positive attitude.

After all, she was a smart woman. A talented woman. A woman on a mission. And she'd succeed. Although it would be a lot easier if she could get Mitch to face her instead of pretending she didn't exist. Maybe her e-mail would help? As soon as she'd gotten back to the resort last night she'd drafted an outline of her pitch, detailing the many reasons why this resort should be themed to cater to the sexual needs of its guests.

Now to see if he responded.

Of course, there were advantages to not dealing with Mitch face-to-face. One of which was wearing jeans and a tank top instead of dressing like a fancy professional. She still wore a crystal-trimmed satin bra under the turquoise silk tank, though. Nothing overt, just a flirty hint of femininity. Her pep talk with Sierra fresh in her mind, she had a solid game plan. Professional and polite, all flirting—except lingerie-style hints—were now off-limits.

That reminder firmly in her head, she gave the manager a finger wave and winked at his trainees as she passed behind the check-in counter to make her way back to Diana's office.

And even though she knew she shouldn't, she gave a little prayer of thanks for her fancy bra when she saw the delicious treat awaiting her.

The only thing better than seeing Mitch Carter first thing in the morning would have been seeing him a little sooner. Like as soon as she'd opened her eyes.

Like her, he wore jeans with his T-shirt. Belle had noticed early on that while the rest of the staff dressed upscale casual, Mitch didn't bother with the upscale part. His rich auburn hair, shoved back off his face, was just past the need-for-a-haircut stage and curling toward his collar.

Her fingers twitched with the desire to touch that hair, to feel it beneath her palms and see if it was as silky and warm as she remembered.

"Mitch," she greeted him with a smile. "This must be my lucky morning."

"Following your lucky night, I suppose."

Belle frowned at the angry snap in his tone, but just shrugged.

"It could have been luckier, of course," she returned, since she'd have much preferred to spend it with him than driving back from L.A. at midnight. "But I had a great time."

"I'll bet."

She made a show of looking around the room, empty but for the two of them. "Just us? I was starting to think that was against the rules or something."

As soon as the words were out, she winced. So much for professional. But, she realized, looking at his stormy face, she was a little hurt at Mitch's blatant avoidance of her, even if he was a total grump-butt in the morning. Someone must have missed his caffeine fix. Belle couldn't recall ever seeing Mitch so out of sorts. It would have been endearing if she didn't feel as if she was blindly stepping into the path of a natural disaster.

"Rules? Don't you just ignore those? Things like showing up to work, agreements and contracts? What, too much like a wedding ceremony for you?"

Anger blasted Belle's amused confusion to bits. She had to grind her teeth to keep from snapping back at him. Lips pressed tightly together, she glared. How dare he?

Mitch arched a brow, challenging her to defend herself.

Belle opened her mouth to yell back, then closed it again, swallowing hard. She hated ugliness and fights. Her parents had fought constantly. Right up until her mother was diagnosed with cancer, every little thing had been an argument. She knew better now, but in second grade, she'd been sure her momma had been argued to death.

Mitch was pissed, most likely because she'd left yesterday. She debated telling him she'd gone to see her father, but didn't see how making him angrier would help anything.

Instead she plastered on her social smile and, with a wink, wiggled her sandal-shod foot toward him. "No sneakers, remember?"

She took his twitching lips as a good sign and opened the leather portfolio she had tucked under her arm. She pulled out the list of local recommendations she'd come up with, along with an outline of the mini events. And, with another glance at the lurking fury in his cinnamon eyes, she steeled her spine and added the theme-pitch outline as well.

"Although both our agreement and contract show these reports due next week," she said, handing them to him, "they're almost complete now and I'd like your input before I go any further. Maybe we can sit down and hammer out some details?"

"I've scheduled the morning to give you the tour you blew off yesterday," he returned.

His words were short, but the curt edge had left his tone. Hearing it gone, Belle felt some of the tension melt from her shoulders.

"Then let's tour," she agreed. "I'm sure I'll have more questions when we're through and we can handle them all at once."

Jaw tight, Mitch gave a stiff nod. Belle hid a sigh. No wonder he and her father had once considered partnership. They were both grumpy SOBs when they wanted to be. Another shock, since she'd have sworn during their engagement that Mitch was the most affable guy in the world. Just went to show how blind she'd been.

"I'll tell Diana we're going," was all he said. But he took the papers with him as he strode into his assistant's office.

Her body tight from the stress of not yelling at his bad-tempered self, Belle dropped into one of the plush chairs outside the main office and heaved a huge sigh. She didn't know which was worse: the way Mitch's irritation pushed her to face her fear of confrontation, or the fact that he was even sexier when he got all intense and uptight like that.

Either way, the man was bad for her control. Part of her wished hard for a pair of sneakers. The other part, the mature businesswoman, steeled her spine and gave thanks that she and Sierra had agreed that professional was the new plan.

An hour later, she was recalling the sports store in town and wondering if sneakers came in pink. Since they'd arrived in the dining room, she'd spent more time sketching pictures of Mitch's butt in her notebook than making notes of the menu plans, rotation of celebrity chefs and floral arrangements.

"Are you getting all of this?" he asked, his words rightfully suspicious. "You look a little distracted."

"The meals I've had since I arrived are excellent, so obviously your chefs are top-notch," she said as if she'd been paying full attention, "but I agree having guest chefs and rotating your menu will keep things fresh. I think, too, that you might want to incorporate some type of theme that works with each chef. For instance, when you bring in the latest Italian wonder, integrate a taste of Italy into the entire month at the resort. Decor, events, that kind of thing."

Mitch's eyes lit up at her suggestion, but he didn't comment. Instead he gestured toward the door and the next stop on their tour. Belle didn't mind, though. She knew she was getting through to him. This was how she liked to do business. Face-to-face. Or, she thought with a tiny sigh as he strode ahead to open the heavy oak door for her, face-to-butt.

God, she wanted him. It was killing her to hold back the flirtation. Instead she kept dropping subtle suggestions and hints that supported her idea to slant the entire resort toward a sexual theme. She wished she could blame her lusty awareness on that, but she knew all the credit went to Mitch.

She reached the door and was surprised, after all his careful avoidance, that Mitch had barely opened it. She had to brush against him to get through. As she did, her eyes met his and she raised a brow.

"The door's stuck," he muttered. "I've got a carpenter coming to look at the hinges."

"Mmm," was all she said. That was the fifth problem they'd encountered so far on the tour. Slipshod construction, a computer failure, a missing stove and, if she hadn't been mistaken, a few too many holes on the golf green.

For a brand-new resort set to open to the public in four weeks, it was a little disconcerting. She knew the hotel business inside-out and a few start-up problems here and there were normal. These seemed excessive.

As they made their way out of the restaurant and toward the

spa and gym, Belle slanted Mitch a sideways glance. She'd thought he was the best. Her daddy had thought so, too, as did everyone she'd talked with. Everybody couldn't be wrong. Could they?

"Do you usually take such a personal hand in your developments, Mitch?" Like the rest of the resort, the mosaic-covered walkway was a combination of art deco and lush greenery. Plants, perhaps echoing the woods beyond the resort, were tucked in every corner, graced every curve. The decor was rich, intense, reminiscent of the Erté statues she'd seen in the foyer.

"My name is on the project, my money is invested in it," he said simply. "I'm going to be involved from the ground up."

Admirable. And, she frowned as she noticed wilting trellis roses, a little concerning. Mitch, who seemed to notice the browned roses at the same time, swore.

"My nana swears that a little water fixes that particular rose problem," Belle joked.

Mitch glared, then pointed to the ground beneath the roses. Belle saw the broken sprinkler heads. Brow furrowed, she stepped closer.

"They look like someone kicked them." A few times, she noted, taking in the destroyed plants surrounding the black plastic. Her first thought was kids, but there were no kids around Lakeside. "Vandals?"

"Maybe. The gardeners keep finding this type of destruction. All minor stuff, just enough to be a pain in the ass."

"This isn't the first vandalism problem?" Construction problems, personnel issues and now vandalism? What was going on? Sure, one or two could be blamed on start-up woes. But all three? Who had Mitch pissed off?

"There've been a few similar landscape issues, along with some missing supplies. The linen shipment disappeared from the laundry room, showed up a week later in the generator shed." The frustration in Mitch's tone was echoed in the cold anger in his eyes. Belle was glad that look wasn't aimed at her. "Nothing I can take to the police as proof there is an actual problem."

"You don't have video out here, right? I remember that being one of the things that factored into my idea to run with the sex theme. You offer so much privacy, it's a shame not to use it. Then again," she waved her hand at the poor rose and wrinkled her nose, "if you're going to waste my plan anyway, maybe you should put in some kind of security measures."

"You have quite a few ideas for someone who can't tear herself away from her hot sex life to do her job," he snapped. "Why don't you focus on not screwing up these events and let me worry about handling my resort."

Belle gasped. Fury such as she'd never felt before flashed hot and bright. She didn't even think to temper it, instead giving in to the wave of anger. "How dare you? Who the hell are you to question my work?"

Normal restraint disappeared, leaving Belle freer than she'd ever felt before. She threw her notebook to the ground, the slap of leather against tile ringing out like a gauntlet.

Two steps was all it took to put her up close and personal with Mitch. Her sandaled toes butted up against his work boots. She glared into his shocked face.

"I'm damned good at my job and have never screwed up a single event. Can you say the same? No," she plowed on before he could respond, "I don't think so. If you have an issue with my work, just say so. Although how you'd have a freaking clue is baffling since all you've done for the last week is hide."

"I—"

She swung her arm up in an arrogant, speak-to-the-hand gesture she'd never thought she'd use and cut him off. Anything he said was only going to piss her off more.

"And for your information, my sex life currently sucks." She slapped her palm against his chest to push him out of her way. She knew it was shock that made him step back, not her strength. She didn't care, as long as he moved. "Just so you know, I blame you for that, too."

MITCH'S MIND reeled between regret at his unfair accusation to astonishment at Belle's reaction. But as she shot that final slap, both physical and verbal, his jaw dropped.

His fault? The hell it was.

Her hair was a silken wave that hit him smack in the face as she spun around to leave. Before she could take more than a step, Mitch grabbed her arm and pulled her back.

Anger, frustration and a pounding desire all beat at him. All the practical excuses and sane reasons he'd taken to reciting daily in an effort to avoid temptation flamed to cinders when he met the fury in her stormy sea-green eyes.

"We need to talk," he said in a low growl. With a quick look at the deserted landscape, he decided it was still too exposed for the chat he had in mind. So, his hand still gripping the soft skin of her arm, he pulled her with him toward the pool's linen room.

"We don't have jack to discuss," she snarled, trying to tug free. "I don't want to talk to you and I guarantee you don't want to hear what I have to say."

"On the contrary," he snapped, pushing the door open and pulling Belle with him into the dimly lit room. It was the size of a small shed. Neatly folded towels filled the shelf-lined walls and the air was warm with the scent of laundry detergent and sunshine. "We obviously have a lot to say to each other."

Belle tugged her arm free and glared. Her breath shuddered in and out, drawing his eyes to the lush bounty he'd been trying to ignore beneath her silky tank top. Mitch's gaze traced the curve of her breasts to the sweet indention of her waist, emphasized by a jeweled belt before the silk gave way to denim.

All week, hell, for the last six years he'd dreamed of her long legs wrapped around him. Of those hips welcoming him. Caution screamed in his head, a blaring warning that he was treading on thin ice. He'd promised that he'd keep his hands off her as long as she worked for him. Too much was at stake.

Apparently unaware of Mitch's inner struggle between desire and his vow to stay the hell out of her pants, Belle planted her fists on her hips, tugging the silk tighter against her breasts in a way that showed a narrow strip of her bra. Sparkling jewels caught the faint light like a treasure beckoning.

"What the hell is your problem?" she asked, her tone as angry as the look on her gorgeous face. "When did you turn into a caveman?"

"We needed to talk," he repeated. "We both have jobs to do. Given all the problems I've had, the last thing I need is you stomping off in a snit."

"Snit?" She actually hissed the word.

Getting turned on by her anger was probably a bad sign.

"Look, I overreacted, okay? But I promised myself I'd keep my hands off you. Which isn't easy with all your blatant flirting and come-ons, I'll have you know."

From the sneer she shot him, it was a piss-poor explanation.

"Want to remind me of when I begged you to put those hands on me?" she asked. She gave him a long, slow, up-and-down look that jacked his already cranked-up libido into full gear. "Did I touch you? A little pat on the ass? Flirty suggestions or come-do-me looks?"

Mitch arched a brow, about to remind her of their first meetings two weeks before. Catching the look, Belle rolled her eyes and flicked her hand toward him. "Bullshit. Anything that happened before we signed our contract doesn't count. You said the only way you'd be comfortable with us working together was if it was all business. I complied."

He hated that she was right. She'd been totally professional. At least she had until she'd blown off the previous day's tour to go on a date. Mitch mentally winced. Was that the real reason for his anger? Was he jealous? Pitiful, especially since he had no right to be.

Mitch's brow furrowed. Damn. It was one thing to be pitiful, but he had no right to take his anger out on her. He ground his teeth and tried to shove the emotion aside. He owed Belle an apology.

Ramming his hands in his pockets, Mitch stiffened his shoulders, battled down the fury and opened his mouth to offer up his apology. Before he could say a word, though, she was off and running again.

"Just because you're too sexually uptight to handle a hot relationship doesn't mean you should take your attitude out on me," she snapped, stabbing at him with her finger.

Mitch's apology turned into a glare but she just rolled her eyes.

"Oh, please. Even if we accept your silly excuse about our past and your business being too touchy to allow anything to happen between us, there's still the rest of it," she scoffed. "Admit it, you're too uptight to consider an incredibly innovative and exciting proposal that would guarantee your resort's success."

He'd had enough. Enough of her accusations. Enough of the sexual frustration that kept him churned up and crazy. Enough of being practical and self-sacrificing for the good of the many.

Screw it all, he was sick and tired of denying himself. For once, he was taking what he wanted.

He gave a low growl. Belle gasped. Before she could do more than blink, he moved, grabbing both her wrists and pinning her, arms overhead, to the smooth wall of the linen shed.

Heat, lust, anger all tangled in his system as he pressed his body close to hers. Like a drug addict grabbing for his fix, he closed his eyes in ecstasy even as he hated himself for giving in to the need.

But damn, it felt good.

Mitch didn't wait for Belle to recover. Instead he took her mouth in an intense, wild kiss. Passion flamed hot and furious between them as she opened her lips to his seeking tongue. Her welcoming moan sent a shaft of desire through him. His downfall felt deliciously decadent.

SHOCK FADED as Belle gave over to the power of Mitch's kiss. She had no idea what had incited the move, but she loved it. Loved the feel of his lips, soft and slick as they moved over hers. The power of his tongue as it tangled and wove, inviting hers to join him in the sensual dance.

Her breath came in pants now. Between the heat of his kiss and the wild excitement of feeling trapped by his hands holding hers prisoner, her panties were damp. She'd never gone for the submission thing, but Mitch holding her captive made her wild to let him have his way with her.

She squirmed a little, needing Mitch to hurry, to do something to relieve the building tension in her belly.

"More," she murmured against his mouth.

"Wait," he murmured back.

She groaned as he slid his lips from hers, already missing the hot dance of his tongue. She sucked in her lower lip, wanting, needing, to taste him.

Mitch traced kisses, hot, wet and exciting, down her throat. Belle groaned when he reached that spot, just there where her neck met her shoulder, and nibbled.

She tugged at her hands, needing to touch him. To feel his shoulders under her fingers, his chest and biceps. She just wanted to grab him and hold on while he took her for a wild ride.

Mitch wouldn't let go. Instead, he shifted so he held both her hands in one of his. Belle thought briefly of how large his hand must be to wrap so neatly around her wrists. The realization made her grin, then, unable to help herself, she pressed her hips closer to his, a quick undulation to check out the myth.

Yummy. If the very hard, very large length pressing against her thigh was any indication, that myth was based on reality. A reality she wanted to see, to feel and get to know up close and personal.

"More," she demanded again. The need in her belly was getting tighter, more urgent. "Quit playing and show me what you've got, big boy."

Mitch chuckled, as she'd hoped he would. But even better, he used his free hand to test the weight of her breast, then in a swift move he released her hands to tug her tank top and bra straps down one shoulder.

Belle's breath caught, her gaze locked on his face. She'd never worried about being judged before, but Mitch was different. She felt she'd wanted him, just like this, all her life. Lust and pure masculine appreciation were clear on his face. That look was as much a turn-on as the feel of his dick, hard and throbbing against her thigh. Tension fled, leaving only desire and need as he met her eyes. Their gazes locked as Mitch traced his finger over her areola, then flicked her hardening nipple.

She gasped.

His gaze dropped to her chest, color heating his cheeks. He bent and touched just the top of his tongue to the aching tip of her breast. Belle wanted to cry at the torment.

But she'd be damned if she'd beg again. Instead she shifted, wrapping one leg around his hip so she could press her wet, hot core against his thigh. The move lifted her breast higher. Mitch showed his appreciation by taking her nipple in his mouth, sucking, licking and nibbling.

Belle whimpered, her breath coming in pants now. Her head fell back against the wall, eyes closed to the dim light as she gave herself over to the wonderful feelings Mitch's mouth was inspiring. She didn't even notice that he'd let go of her wrists until she felt one hand under her butt. That hand lifted, controlled her undulations as he pressed her closer. The other tugged the second bra strap down to bare both breasts.

His mouth still tormenting one nipple, he worked the other with his fingers. Belle groaned her approval, pressing tight enough that the seam of her jeans added to the spiraling pleasure.

Mitch released his grip on her butt, shifting just a little so Belle could wrap both legs around his hips, his dick pressed against her throbbing core. The denim between them only added to her wild excitement.

Holding a breast in each large hand, he pressed them together. His thumbs worked her nipples as his mouth moved, wet and wild, first tormenting the left, then the right. Belle's hips jerked. She pressed closer, her ankles grabbing tight to his butt.

Heaven. When he nipped, teeth sharp yet gentle, at her wet nipple, she cried out in pleasure and lost control.

Gasping for breath, she came hard and fast. Lights exploded behind her eyes, her body melted with the power of the orgasm.

"Ohmygod, ohmygod, ohmygod," she chanted as she rode the wave. Mitch kept her up there, his tongue still working, his hand back beneath her butt to support her as she collapsed in delight.

Tension—hell, all feeling—fled her body as she sank into the afterglow of a first-class orgasm. Her legs numb, she dropped her feet to either side of Mitch's, but didn't shift away from the throbbing power of his dick where it pressed against her belly.

It took her a minute to realize he'd stopped his torment of her breasts. When she did, she lifted her head and opened her eyes to meet his.

She had to laugh. His grin was pure male ego.

Then it faded. Belle heard voices outside and realized his crew had probably shown up to fix the sprinkler problem.

Seeing she'd regained control, Mitch stepped away, visibly working to regulate his breathing. Belle stared through foggy eyes, satisfaction throbbing in her belly, between her legs. Damn, she felt great.

"Your turn?" she asked, her voice husky with pleasure.

She watched him swallow, then glance out the narrow window.

"The last thing I need my gardeners seeing is my bare ass," he said with a grimace.

Belle smirked. The chances of the gardeners peeking in were slim at best, but she didn't bother calling him on the flimsy excuse.

"I'm not uptight," he insisted. Belle kept silent, letting her arched brow speak volumes.

Well, he hadn't *felt* uptight, that was for sure. But then, he hadn't dropped his drawers, either. Rather than giving him the agreement he so obviously wanted, she just shrugged and adjusted her clothing, again not saying anything.

She hid her grin when she heard his teeth grinding from across the tiny shed.

"I'll read your proposal again," he suddenly promised. Shocked, Belle met his eyes. "If it's as solid as I remember, I'll submit it to my management team."

She didn't want a job—any job—based on sex, or in Mitch's case, unrequited sexual need. But she did want a chance.

"Why?" she asked.

"Because you're right. The idea is solid, it meshes with what I'm trying to do here. So it's worth considering."

"And if your team agrees?"

"We'll modify your contracts."

Belle nodded. Then she moved forward, close enough to feel the assurance that he was still hot, hard and excited. "And what about us?"

Mitch winced. "It'd be stupid to screw up a business deal over sex."

"It doesn't have to be like that," she returned, noticing he didn't say they wouldn't have sex. "Think of it this way. My proposal for your resort is based on sexual thrills. Don't you owe it to your clientele to try them all first?"

Mitch's eyes went round, then crinkled with laughter. "Why don't we see how the proposal goes first?"

Belle grimaced, thinking of what the last proposal between them had cost her. But she was smarter this time and definitely nowhere near as naive.

With that in mind, she gave Mitch her most wicked grin and stepped closer, letting the back of her fingers brush over his still-straining erection.

"You take me up on my proposal—business, pleasure or both—and I promise, you won't regret it."

With that and a quick butterfly kiss, she turned to saunter away. She felt the heat of his gaze on her swaying hips and let her grin fall away. Now she'd better figure out how to make damned sure *she* didn't regret it, either.

6

"WHAT KIND of sexy food did you have in mind for the room-service menu?" Mitch asked the people around the board table. This was their first group brainstorming session on the resort's new theme and he wasn't doing so well. It was a struggle to use the same tone he'd employ to discuss the type of artwork they'd carry in the lobby or how many brands of scotch the bar should have on hand. In other words, to keep this discussion at the level of pure business.

Damned hard, too, seeing the woman sitting across from him who had cried his name as he brought her to an orgasm in a towel closet three days before. The look she was giving him, pure flirtatious amusement, told him she was waiting for a repeat performance.

"Probably just two or three items," Belle said, her delight at the conversation, and probably at his apparent discomfort, clear in her tone. "The trick is going to be choosing the right ones. You might want to tie into your revolving-guest-chef theme with these. Keep a standard on the menu at all times, say oysters, since their reputation is so tried in food."

Mitch exchanged confused frowns with his manager, then asked, "Tried and true?"

"Exactly." She shot him a grin before leaning over to dig through her satchel and pull out files for everyone at the table. Their current discourse on sexual turn-ons was being shared with two of his managers, his head chef Jacques, and Miles, the resort's head of security. A nice, intimate group with which to brainstorm kink.

Belle had put them all at their ease, though. From the minute she'd walked into the room in her demure black skirt and red sleeveless turtleneck, she'd had his staff in the palm of her delectable little hand. A couple of jokes, a personal comment to each guy to let him know she'd done her research and appreciated the job he did, and they'd all relaxed.

And, given the topic, relaxation was key. At first, nobody had wanted to jump in with an opinion, so it'd been just Mitch and Belle talking sex. But after a quarter of an hour or so, the group hadn't been able to hold back. Now the opinions and ideas were flowing fast and furious, which gave Mitch time to sit back and watch Belle at work.

He glanced at the list she'd handed out. Title: Aphrodisiacs. He couldn't help but laugh. Belle winked at him.

"The room-service menu should otherwise be standard, of course." She glanced around the table and all the men nodded in agreement. Mitch suspected they'd have nodded if she'd suggested adding popcorn and Popsicles to the menu, they were so equally fascinated and out of their element. "But for the restaurant menu we can get more creative. Maybe cultural or thematic—Mexican chocolate, oysters Rockefeller, Greek honey cakes. That kind of thing."

"Graphic desserts?" offered Larry.

"Too bachelorette partyesque," Belle rejected with a grimace. "Think classier. Something that convinces people this isn't a gimmick, that it will really work."

"Asparagus and arugula salad?" he offered.

"There you go," she said, pointing her pen at him in approval before making note of his suggestion.

Mitch snickered when Larry preened as though he'd just been given a gold star.

Damn, she was good. She definitely knew what she was doing. Her society-princess title had been well earned. She orchestrated the meeting like a cocktail party, introducing this idea and that, making sure everyone had a chance to interject their comments before rearranging and serving the concepts back to them on a platter.

Who knew watching a sexy woman using her brain to work a room could be such a turn-on. Mitch wasn't a chauvinist pig, he respected women for more than their bodies. But he'd had no idea Belle had so much more going on.

He thought back to their engagement. He'd never seen her as a real person, just a princess to be won. And then there was their towel-closet encounter. While she'd obviously enjoyed the end results, he doubted she was impressed with his finesse and gentlemanly behavior.

Mitch grimaced. Maybe he was a pig.

"Now that we've covered the menu, let's see if we can nail a few of the special amenity details," Belle suggested, launching the discussion in a whole different direction.

Since most of those details were sexually explicit, Mitch had to work to keep his expression neutral.

"Do you really think handcuffs are necessary?" he asked as Diana brought in a tray of coffee and snacks. Apparently Belle had left word that she needed a midafternoon pick-me-up and his assistant was only too happy to oblige. Mitch couldn't say he blamed Diana, since he'd willingly do quite a few things, most cheap and kinky, to see Belle's smile of gratitude flash his way.

"Of course you need handcuffs," Belle said, her green eyes flashing wicked delight at odds with her matter-of-fact tone. "The key to having this work is to keep the sexual offerings classy by making them a standard amenity. If a guest has to call down to the concierge and ask for sex toys, it ruins the spontaneity."

From the bemused looks on the faces his staff as Belle passed around a tray of cookies, Mitch figured they were as speechless at that image as he was.

"And our goal is spontaneous sex?" he finally asked, giving up all pretense that he wasn't completely out of his element.

"That is precisely our goal," Belle said, her eyes hot and intense as she nibbled at a chocolate cookie. "The more spontaneous, and the more sex, the better."

Mitch went from intrigued to rock-hard in two seconds flat.

"You'll need to specially train your front desk and your concierge," Belle continued, talking to Larry. "Given the target demographic, you want to support the high-end thrill and excitement of a sexual getaway. Few people looking for the privacy to indulge their sexual fantasies care to explain to a concierge whether they prefer their handcuffs fur-lined or solid metal."

"Good point." Mitch frowned as he made a note on his report and muttered, "Apparently I'm going to need to find a supplier of kinky toys."

Belle pulled a paper from her file and handed him a complete list of companies, color-coded by fetish.

Helpless to do otherwise, Mitch snorted with laughter. Damn, she was good. Belle shot him an impish smile that said she knew what he was thinking and looked forward to proving just how good she could be.

BELLE LEFT Mitch's boardroom, doing a little happy dance as soon as the door swung shut behind her.

"That went well, I take it?" Diana asked, a hint of something Belle didn't understand in her tone.

"It was fabulous," Belle returned, too curious about the

other woman to feel embarrassed. "I think this is going to rock. Everyone had great ideas. It's got success written all over it."

From Diana's grimace-faking-it-as-a-smile, Belle figured the other woman might have some issues with the sex stuff. Leave it to Mitch to hire a prude as his assistant, Belle thought affectionately. But she'd brought him around, and she was sure she could bring Diana to accept the concept as well.

With that in mind, she pulled a chair up close to the woman's desk and leaned forward with her friendliest look.

"This must be fascinating," she said conversationally. "Being in on the ground floor of opening such a great place. I mean, you're surrounded by luxury, an incredible view and a hot boss. And once the place is open, it'll be like free cable. The inside scoop on famous people and clandestine sex. Not a bad job, huh?"

Diana looked at her as if she was a two-headed dog and both sides were missing a brain. Uptight *and* no sense of humor? Poor Mitch.

"Or not," Belle muttered, wondering if she had any common ground with this woman. She surveyed Diana's polyester blouse, navy slacks and flat pleather sandals. Probably not.

Belle glanced at her watch and sighed. How much longer was Mitch going to be?

"So tell me, Diana, how's the resort shaping up?" she asked after a few minutes of miserably uncomfortable silence. She didn't really care about the answer but was desperate for some conversation.

"Falling apart is more like it," the other woman mumbled into her computer screen.

"Beg pardon?"

Diana slanted her a sideways look and shrugged. "You know, it's just one problem after another. I've never been in on the—how did you say it?—ground floor of a resort opening before. But I'd imagined it'd be a little smoother, if you know what I mean."

Belle's brows shot up. "You mean things like the sprinklers and construction hitches?"

Diana winced. "Sure, those and the gophers and the computer crashes and the laundry mix-up and the lost supplies and, well, I could keep going but you get my drift."

Funny how the woman lost her quiet reserve when she was reciting all the resort's issues. Belle frowned and gave a one-shouldered shrug. "I'm sure that's all part and parcel to opening a new venue."

At least, she assumed it was. Her father's hotels had never hit so many hitches, but then he'd been at it a long time. This was Mitch's first hospitality venue, so maybe he just hadn't found his stride yet?

"Maybe," Diana agreed doubtfully. "I mean, I've heard such amazing things about Mr. Carter. He's got a reputation for being such an expert."

Diana's tone made it clear that she wasn't buying the rep any longer. Doubt washed over Belle. Was Mitch the guy to help her dad? She'd been so sure. As Diana said, he had a stellar reputation for being Mr. Amazing when it came to business. She frowned. Was that rep wrong?

"Can you excuse me for a minute," she asked Diana. "If Mitch comes out, just let him know I had a call I forgot I have to make."

"You can make it here," Diana said, pointing to the phone.

"Um, no thanks." Belle waved her cell phone and gestured toward the hallway. "It's…private."

The other woman gave her an ohhh-one-of-those-calls look and shrugged.

Once alone, Belle punched a button and paced impatiently while waiting for Sierra to pick up.

"We might need to rethink a few things," she said as soon as her partner answered.

"Which few?"

Belle explained the resort issues she'd discovered, both on her own and the ones Diana had shared. "So now I'm wondering if Mitch is really the right guy to help daddy."

"What about the Eventually Yours gig? Do we need to pull out?"

Pull out? Belle considered the question. They couldn't. They'd tied up a lot of time and energy in this project. If it went belly-up, they would definitely hurt. But not enough for her to consider ditching Mitch. He believed in the resort and had so much more at stake. She wanted to give him her support, even if he didn't realize it. The only thing she was risking was her time and energy. Yes, Eventfully Yours might take a hit, but as long as she came up with some other idea to help her dad, she could handle it.

"I gave my word, I can't back out." Her fear of failure faded a little as she made the statement.

At Sierra's snort she pulled the phone away from her ear and rolled her eyes.

"I've matured," she claimed, talking into the speaker again.

"Matured my ass. You just want to get in his pants."

"That's beside the point," Belle mumbled. So what if she did? Was that the only reason she wanted to stick with the job? No, of course not. She believed in it. She'd had a great time in their brainstorming session and the ideas they'd all come up with were awesome.

With that in mind, she squared her shoulders, shook off her nerves and claimed, "This is business and we signed a contract. Besides, I really haven't seen any hard evidence to make me believe Mitch isn't all his reputation says. Just little things that could easily be chalked up to normal start-up woes."

"You wouldn't have called me if you weren't worried."

"Not worried. Cautiously concerned about the big picture, you know?" And she hadn't wanted to voice her doubts about Mitch's success aloud. It seemed so disloyal.

"You mean you don't want to let your lust for this guy blind you a second time."

Belle pulled a face and, feeling like a slug, mumbled, "I'd rather just depend on us, if you know what I mean. As long as you're okay with the decision."

Sierra was silent for a second. Belle heard the cellophane crinkle of a candy wrapper. Then, "Eventfully Yours can handle whatever happens. The real question is, what do you want to do about your dad? Find someone else to help him? Like who? You're the one with all the hotel experience."

Blinking away tears of relief at her friend's understanding and support, Belle paced and considered. "Let's just see what we can come up with ourselves, okay? I don't want to make any decisions yet. I just, you know, needed a sounding board and to get your brain in on the action."

"What are you going to do while my brain works?"

Mitch strode out of his office just then. Unlike the businessmen her daddy worked with, who always did the suit-and-tie thing, Mitch seemed to have left that phase behind him. Other than their meeting at the restaurant when they'd signed the contracts, he always wore jeans.

As Mitch turned to respond to something Diana had said, Belle sighed. Damn, she loved a guy in jeans.

"Continue with plan A," Belle said as her eyes met Mitch's when he turned around.

"Jump his bones?" Sierra confirmed.

"You know it." With that, Belle pushed the disconnect button and slid her phone into her bag.

"Ready?" Mitch asked, referring to their plans to tour the golf course and wooded picnic area.

"I need to change," she said, waving her high-heeled sandal-clad foot his way. "Let's stop by my room and I'll get some flats, okay?"

They headed outside toward her cottage.

"I don't think I ever saw you in jeans when we were dating or engaged," she commented.

Mitch's look of surprise must be due to her bringing up the past, Belle figured. But while she wasn't about to play the blame game, it was silly to pretend they didn't have a past. Maybe if they melted the ice with easy chit-chat, she'd be able to work up the nerve to apologize for abandoning him at the altar before her job here was done.

"Six years ago I had too much to prove to let myself wear jeans," Mitch finally said.

Intriguing. "And did you?"

"Did I what?"

"Prove your point? And what was it? That denim makes your ass look great, but you wanted to be taken seriously so you denied the world the sweet sight?"

He snorted and shook his head. They'd reached her cottage, so he gestured for her to precede him to the door. Belle glanced back to see if he was going to answer and caught him checking out *her* ass. She grinned. Well, tit for tat and all that.

"Hardly," he said, shrugging an apology for the ogling. Belle just winked back to let him know she didn't mind. "I wanted to play with the big boys. Hotels, entertainment. I figured nobody would take a hammer-swinging kid seriously so I went the businessman route."

"Trying to be a wolf with silk ears?"

He frowned, then after a second corrected, "Wolf in sheep's clothing? Or silk purse out of a sow's ear?"

"Both." She smiled up at him as she pushed open the door. "But I heard talk before you showed up in those fancy suits. Nobody thought of you as a kid or as less than a driving force. They were looking forward to working with you. You had a great rep."

At least he had before she got a hold of him. Belle winced and, before he could respond by pointing out that exact fact, she gestured to the bowl of fruit on the small kitchenette table. "Help yourself to a snack while I change, hmm?"

And off she scurried, like a scared little mouse, guilt pounding at her like a sledgehammer on speed. In the bedroom, she dropped to her bed and stared at the ceiling while reciting all the reasons she'd screwed up and why he had the right to hold them against her. Then, once they were out of her system, she shot up and tugged open the plantation-style closet doors to grab a denim skirt and casual blouse for their tour.

MITCH BLINKED at the closed door, wondering what the hell had just happened. One second he and Belle had been having a friendly jaunt into the past. The next she was offering him a banana and running away.

Apparently that was the theme of their relationship, that running thing.

He sighed and glanced around the cottage. *California casual* was the term the decorator had used—light woods, soft fabric, bare tile floors. The space was open and airy with a few plants here and there to make it welcoming. As comfortable as it had started out, in less than a week, Belle had made it her own.

Colorful scarves over the chairs added rich splashes of green and turquoise. A wooden bowl filled with engraved stones sat on the coffee table. Mitch walked over to pick one out. *Perseverance,* he read. Motivational sayings? Belle?

He noticed a small framed poster on the wall. Stone in hand, he stepped closer to read about the ABCs to Achieve Your Dreams.

Wild. He frowned at the closed door and tried to adjust his image of her, a flighty sexpot with great planning skills, with the idea that she bought, let alone used, motivational tools.

It was then that he saw it. A small, fluffy, pink, stuffed

bunny rabbit. As spotless as the day he'd won it for her at a corporate fund-raising carnival, it sat in the rocking chair looking fat and content.

Mitch grinned at the sight and, tossing the stone back in the bowl, lifted the bunny for a closer look.

"Don't mess with Mr. Winkles," Belle said, coming out of the bedroom. Her tone was light, but there was still a lingering frown around her eyes.

"I can't believe you still have this," he said with a laugh, holding up the stuffed animal. "I never took you for the sentimental type." He considered, then added, "I never thought our time together was something worthy of sentiment, to tell you the truth."

As soon as the words were out, Mitch winced. He sounded like an ass. But, well, the truth was, he'd never allowed himself to think about their time together as anything but a business deal gone bad. It hurt less that way.

She gave him the glare of death, but in a blink, the look was gone. Had he imagined it? Maybe.

Then she snatched the toy from his hands as if he'd stolen it. That's when it hit him.

"Are you embarrassed?" he asked with a grin. "There's no reason to be. I think it's sweet."

Her porcelain skin flushed crimson and the death glare returned in full force. She gripped one hand so tightly around the rabbit's neck, it'd be stew meat if it wasn't a stuffed toy. Mitch winced. From the look on her face, she was imagining his throat between her fingers.

"Sweet, my ass," she shot back. "I'm not sentimental over our time together. Believe me, the last thing I need is a constant reminder of my mistake."

Mitch's spine snapped straight, his amusement fleeing at that one word. *Mistake.*

Oh, yeah, there had been mistakes. But they were his. It'd taken him six years to make up for the business ones, and damned if he needed his personal ones thrown in his face by the woman at fault for all of them.

"Mistake? Care to clarify that?" he asked, his tone the one he reserved for embezzlers, liars and cheats. Icy-cold and precise.

"Oh please, like you don't know." Her sneer was a work of art. Angry, but still disdainful enough to hide the hurt he'd glimpsed earlier. And he'd called her sentimental? "You can pretend all you want that we're business buddies here, but we both know damned well what happened."

"Us and a couple of hundred guests," he shot back.

Belle rolled her eyes. "That's your own damned fault," she declared. "If you hadn't put such an insane price on your body, we'd never have ended up in that mess."

Mitch had fallen off a fifth-story girder once, his safety rope keeping him from serious injury. That was the only time he recalled ever being this close to speechless. He stared, mouth open. "My body?"

"I wanted sex," she declared, pointing the bunny at him like a pistol. "Simple, uncomplicated sex. But no, you had to turn it into something else. Complicate it. You ruined everything, and for what? Ambition?" Disdain dripped from her words like battery acid, burning Mitch.

He clenched his jaw, struggling to find a response. Anger pounded at his temples: fury at the past and at the woman in front of him for reminding him that he'd never measured up.

He'd spent his entire career trying to prove himself. To prove he was man enough to take care of his mother after his dad had died. To prove he was worthy of the trust his stepfather had later showed in him. And then to prove that he wasn't going to fall apart when he'd been left with the responsibility of his stepdad's construction company.

And then he finally thought he'd found his perfect woman. The one he'd seen as proof that he was man enough for anything. And she'd walked out on him.

Mitch had never admitted, not to anyone but himself in the dark hours when it was just him and his thoughts, his fears that Belle had found him lacking. That she'd decided he wasn't rich enough, wasn't talented enough, wasn't worthy enough.

It was the last one that really grated. All he'd wanted from the moment he'd set eyes on the sassy blond was to sweep her off her feet.

Mitch glared at her, all grown up now and just as sassily sexy. He should have swept when he had a chance. Maybe if he'd knocked her feet out from under her she wouldn't have run away.

Well, he'd blown his chance once. He wasn't stupid enough to blow it twice.

"You wanted sex?" he ground out, anger and lust sharp and jagged in his system. "Fine, I'll give you sex."

Two steps was all it took to pin her between the hard, needy length of his body and the wall. Belle's shocked gasp was lost against his mouth. Her sea-green eyes glared into his as she gave a low growl. Being a smart man, Mitch kept his tongue out of the game just yet. But he used his lips to full effect.

And his hands. Because, if he did say so himself, he was damned good with his hands. He skimmed them over her hair, a gentle glide down her shoulders then a quick, barely-there flick along the sides of her full breasts, crushed against his chest. He gripped the gentle curve of her waist for just a second, then gave in to the need and scooped his hands under the sweet curve of her ass.

Mitch groaned as the move pressed her tighter to the throbbing length of his dick. God, he wanted her.

Tossing off all restraint, all the rules he'd tried so hard to live by, he let himself go. His hands gripped Belle's butt, squeezing her soft curves one more time before he pulled her between his thighs. One hand slid up to cup the back of her neck, holding her head in place when she tried to jerk away from his kiss.

Feeling her heart pounding in her throat, he told himself it was passion and, desperately needing to taste her, he risked it all and slid his tongue along the seam of her full, soft lips.

Her shuddered gasp was barely discernable, but he felt it. Both against his mouth, and in the way she pressed herself tighter against his erection. Her wiggle was a tiny thing, but damn, it felt great. His grin was fast and triumphant before he took her mouth in a wild ride. Tongues dueled and tangled in a dance of passion. Quick, deep kisses that hinted at dark pleasures and intense emotion. He gave over to the power of tasting her, feeling her. Belle, the one obsession he'd never been able to shake.

A voice whispered in the back of his head to slow down. Mitch told the voice to shut the hell up. In pure defiance he shifted her, one quick move, to straddle his hips and gave a guttural groan when she wrapped those long, delicious legs around him. Mitch pressed, once, twice. Belle mimicked his rhythm, taking on the slow, intense undulation.

Desperate now, he released her hip and neck to cup her breasts. The heated warmth filled his palm. Her soft whimper turned to a moan when he flicked his thumbs over her pebbled nipples.

Need pounded now, a heavy dark beat. Mitch gave in to it, releasing her mouth as he pulled her blouse over her head. Seconds before he lost himself in the lush bounty of her breasts, he met her eyes. Head supported by the wall, her blond hair a cloudy pillow behind her, Belle stared back. Desire, power, pleasure all shone in her gaze.

Mitch's ultimate dream, here in his hands, the taste of her rich on his tongue. The image he had of him and Belle—the poor kid in patched jeans and the princess—flashed through his head. *You've come a long way, baby,* that voice said. But, he vowed, not nearly as long as he planned to make Belle come.

7

WHO KNEW confrontation could feel so good? Belle's breath trembled, the wall a hard pillow behind her head, and she closed her eyes and let the delicious sensations wash over her in powerful, throbbing waves.

Her fingers slid, caressing their way through Mitch's hair as she pressed his face closer to her breasts. The contrast of his mouth, so soft and moist and warm, and his cheek, roughening just hours after his morning shave, drove her nuts.

Fingers stroked, squeezed, in rhythm with her movements. Belle hitched just a little so her skirt shifted up higher, out of the way. Ahhh, she pressed closer, her silk panties moist and hot. They added to the intensity of his rough jeans against her swollen nether lips.

She wanted to squirm, to ratchet up the power. She wanted hard and fast and intense blood-pounding sex against the wall.

But Mitch was in charge, and despite the wall and the absolute control he'd grabbed early on, he was taking it slow. Damn him.

With deliberate care, he scraped his teeth over her aching nipples. Belle gasped and gripped his hair tighter, needing more. His tongue swirled, taunted and teased the tip of one breast, then switched to the other to continue the torment. Belle ground herself against the hard length of him.

"More," she moaned.

"Soon," he said, his breath hot against her damp flesh. Belle squirmed again, losing the rhythm. Her frantic movement made Mitch groan, the smooth stroke of his tongue turning to an almost desperate sucking motion.

Oh, yeah. Heat, fast and furious, shot through her body like a bolt of lightning. Pleasure bordered on pain as his mouth ravaged her breast, his hand gripping the other in a heated caress. Yeah, that's what she wanted. Her head fell back again, her eyes closed as she gave herself over to the sensations. Her panties were soaked now as she rode up and down the rigid length of his turgid, zipper-covered dick.

"I'm not doing this alone—again," she panted. "This time I want you with me."

"I'm right here."

"Naked," she insisted. She'd spent six-plus years wanting to get her hands on his naked body and she didn't want to wait a second more. "I want to see you. Touch you. Taste you."

He groaned and gave a little shudder, but didn't stop.

"After," he said.

After?

Mitch shifted, bringing one hand down between their bodies while the other still caressed the nipple he wasn't sucking. His fingers stroked the wet silk between her legs, sending a jolt of pleasure through her. Belle gasped, her thighs trembling as he worked her swollen clitoris through the fabric.

He played her body like a virtuoso, bringing her higher and higher with every flick of his tongue, brush of his fingers. As her climax built, she knew which "after" he was referring to.

Then he slid the fabric of her panties out of the way. He danced his fingers over her slick folds, pressing, sliding, driving her crazy. Stars danced behind Belle's closed eyes, her body on overload. Mitch's tongue teased her nipple, then sucked it deep into his mouth as he worked her with his fingers.

One finger in, then out, was all it took. Belle exploded. Her thighs tightened, her fingers grabbed Mitch's shoulders as the orgasm shook her body. Spirals of pleasure danced through her system, spinning higher, wilder as she flew over the edge.

She slowly floated back to earth, her breath soft pants as she became aware of Mitch again. His mouth pressed into the curve of her throat, he held her tight against his body. As her thoughts coalesced, she felt the tension and strain in his shoulders, the bunched muscles of his back. And, she realized, that ever so deliciously hard muscle throbbing behind his zipper.

Twice now he'd made her come with all her clothes on, not taking anything in return. While she wouldn't deny the thrill of being taken against the wall—twice—she still wanted a little more active role in screwing Mitch's brains out.

With that in mind, as soon as she thought they'd hold her, she let her legs slide down Mitch's hard thighs, sighing at the sensation of denim against bare flesh. Feet on the floor, she felt her knees try to buckle, making Belle grateful to be sandwiched between the wall and Mitch's body.

Time to upgrade this event to a couples theme…

"Off," Belle purred, needing to feel skin. Years. She'd waited years for this opportunity and she'd be damned if she was going to waste a single second of it. Not even to bask in the afterglow of a rockin' orgasm.

Her hands slid up his forearms, the soft hair tickling her palms. As she passed over the rolled-up chambray sleeves, she paused to squeeze his rock-solid biceps. She wanted to see those muscles. Now. She pulled at Mitch's shirt to get it out of her way. Buttons flew everywhere. She didn't care. Her eyes were focused on the prize, on the broad planes of his smooth, golden chest.

"Mmm," she murmured as she took in the sight. She let Mitch deal with getting the shirt off his arms. She was busy appreciating the view. Golden skin stretched over the nicest set of pecs she'd seen since ogling the big screen. Like the first fall leaves, a dusting of mahogany hair trailed down his chest. Belle swallowed, her eyes landing on the very large, very hard package pressing against the worn denim of his jeans. Yowza and come to momma. She placed one hand against his hard chest while she smoothed the other over his shoulder, down that bicep again. Mitch wrapped his hands around her waist, but she barely noticed his caress, so focused was she on the tactile wonderland of his body.

She leaned forward, pressing her face to the warmth of his chest, breathing in his cologne, then turned her head just a little to flick her tongue over his flat nipple. He swiftly sucked in his breath, his abs going concave.

Belle grinned her appreciation before letting her head fall back to look into his face.

"You're gorgeous," she told him. "Sexy, buff and delicious. I plan to taste every single inch of you."

His eyes seemed to lose their focus at her words. Releasing her waist, he shoved his hands into her hair, fingers gripping the back of her scalp. He pulled her up to meet his mouth. Hot and wild, his tongue ravaged hers. Belle wasn't about to give up control, though, so she met him thrust for thrust, then sucked his tongue into her mouth in a way that made him groan and reach for her naked breasts.

"No," she gasped, moving away before he could work his magic and distract her again. "My turn."

And she made the most of it. In little, nibbling bites and long wet kisses, she worked her way over his chest and down his belly.

Dropping to her knees, she pressed her cheek against the bulge in his jeans and, glancing up to give him a wicked grin, reached around to squeeze his butt. Mitch's laugh eased her tension, and with an answering wink she released the catch on his pants and eased his zipper down.

A quick shove was all it took to bare his straining dick, right there at mouth level. She sighed in appreciation at the sight, sure that very tasty treat was going to bring her untold hours of pleasure.

Like a yummy lollipop, she ran her tongue up the length of his shaft and grinned when he grabbed her shoulders and groaned. Oh, yeah, she was definitely going to enjoy this. With a sigh of pleasure, she wrapped her lips around the smooth cap, and after a couple of teasing swirls of her tongue, quit playing and gave him the best head she could.

After a couple minutes of service, Mitch's fingers dug into her shoulders in a gentle signal that he was reaching his limit. She briefly considered pushing him over that limit, sending him right off the cliff, but then realized there were so many more delights to be had. Why rush things?

With a smooth slurping motion, she released him and leaned back on her hands. Mitch watched her like a man possessed, waiting to see what her next move would be, a wicked grin playing at the corner of his mouth.

"How're you at numbers?" she asked, her breath shuddering as the spiraling heat reignited in her belly. Pressing her fingers against her damp, aching mound, she pulled them away to show him the wet evidence of her desire.

"You mean like sixty-nine?" At her nod, Mitch reached down and took her hand, dropping to his knees as well and sucking her fingers into his mouth. Belle whimpered at the action, the tension between her legs ratcheting even higher. "I'm damned good, as you're about to find out," he promised.

"Do that again," she instructed, "just, you know, somewhere else."

Mitch's grin flashed. In a quick move, he kicked off his

shoes, tugged his socks and jeans off, too. Naked, he lay back on the floor and gestured.

"Gimme," he said. "But get naked first."

Belle glanced down at herself—on her knees, her blouse long gone, her bra scooped under her breasts, pressing them up and together in a way that made them look much larger than they actually were. Her skirt was bunched around her waist like a belt, and her panties but a tattered memory of silk and lace.

She stood, placing one foot on either side of Mitch's hips and giving him a clear view of her wet, pink folds. Like a magnet, his eyes flew to the sight and his grin fell away. He reached for her but she shook her head, so he settled on running his hands up and down her calves, accented by the high heels she still wore.

She smoothed her skirt back in place. He frowned, then watched as she flipped the hook and zipper open. Belle shimmied, her breasts swaying with the movement. Mitch's eyes went opaque. She pushed the tight skirt down her hips, and bending one knee to bring her legs together, she dropped the skirt to the floor, then kicked it away.

Almost naked now and loving Mitch's full attention, Belle stood, legs spread, and gently scraped her nails up her thighs. She passed her hand over the damp curls between her legs, pausing to flick one finger over her clit. The movement made Mitch's dick jump as though it was jealous. She loved his eyes on her. It was almost as good as his hands, although not nearly as sweet as his mouth. She felt like a sex goddess, the way he looked at her. She slid her hands up her torso, cupping her breasts and squeezing them. Head falling back, she closed her eyes and let the sensation, hot, intense and powerful, wash over her.

Her fingers tweaked her aching, turgid nipples, amping up her desire, preparing her for the thrust of Mitch's tongue. As if he heard her thoughts, suddenly his mouth was between her legs. Belle gasped, then gave a keening cry as he skipped all the preliminaries and thrust his tongue inside her.

Her knees buckled again, but his hands were there on her ass to hold her up. She looked down and almost came at the sight. Her nails teased and circled the pointy pink tips of her nipples, and there below Mitch half sat, half lay, his eyes staring into hers as he used his tongue to drive her crazy.

She wanted to come. Two more seconds and she would. But she'd promised herself the next time she'd be taking him down with her. Calling on a willpower she'd have sworn didn't exist, she stepped away from the best tongue job she'd ever had and pointed to the floor. Mitch frowned. Belle arched her brow. Not bothering to take off her shoes, she gestured to the floor again and ran her hands over her breasts in promise.

Mitch lay back, his dick as rigid as a redwood, waiting for her. As gracefully as possible, Belle dropped down, one knee on either side of his hips. Her wet bush rubbed against his dick, tempting her to simply shift and take him inside her. But she wanted more, she wanted to drive him so crazy he never forgot her. She wanted him to want her so bad, she became the most important thing in his life. Even if it was only for the moment.

Needing the connection, she let herself fall forward so her hands braced on either side of his head, and kissed him. Dark and drugging, the kiss tasted like musky sex.

With one last bite at his lower lip, she sat upright, then swung her legs around so she faced backward. Falling forward to brace her elbows on the floor on either side of his hips, she wrapped one hand around the base of his straining dick and, knowing he was waiting, feeling the tension in him building, swirled her tongue over the silky head. Mitch groaned and grabbed her hips, his fingers digging erotically into the soft flesh. She swirled again, then pulled just the head into her mouth, sucking it like a lollipop. He got even harder and she felt him groan, a warm gust of air between her thighs. Then his mouth was on her. He licked, then sucked her clit into his mouth, causing Belle to shudder.

Determined to make him come first, and hanging on to her control by the thinnest thread, she poured everything she had into giving him the best, the hottest and sexiest blow job of her life. Lips, teeth and tongue worked magic as she sucked and swirled, taking him deeper. His tongue mimicked lovemaking, spearing her in then out, as his finger massaged her swollen lips.

Belle couldn't take much more. While still sucking, she scraped her teeth, gentle as could be, up the length of him. Mitch stiffened and grabbed her hips. She did it again. His fingers tightened, then proving those rock-hard biceps were well-deserved, he lifted and flipped her around so she faced him.

He reached up and wrapped his hand around the back of her neck, pulling her mouth down to meet his. Wet, sliding, open-mouth kisses added to the intense, needy ache in her belly. While driving her crazy, Mitch reached over to pull his jeans to him and grabbed a condom out of his pocket.

Releasing her mouth, he let his head fall back to the carpet and handed her the foil packet. "Ride me," he demanded.

In quick moves made jerky by impatience and need, she sheathed his straining erection in the ribbed-for-her-pleasure condom and rose to her knees.

One leg on either side of his hips, she locked eyes with Mitch. Excruciatingly slowly, she lowered herself one delicious inch at a time on his rock-hard cock until she'd taken all of him inside her.

With a shuddering moan, she ran her hands up the sides of her body, her skin so sensitized the barely-there move made her want to scream with pleasure. She slid her hands over her breasts and up her throat, then speared them through her hair. Lifting her arms overhead, she gave silent thanks for the delicious treat she was about to enjoy.

Then she set out to pleasure the hell out of herself. Riding him, slowly at first and with ever-increasing strokes, she let the tension build. Tighter, deeper, need coiled low in her belly. Belle's gaze stayed locked on Mitch's, watching his eyes to gauge his pleasure. Fingers meshed as they held hands, their focus completely, totally on the sensations building in both of them as Belle rode him.

Her climax just a breath away, her body started to shake as she tried to hold off. She needed to see him come first. Had to know she could give him as much pleasure as he gave her. With that in mind, trying as hard as she could to hold off the pounding orgasmic waves, she swirled her hips, adding a deep undulating move to each thrust.

Mitch's eyes went dark, then closed for a second as he fought for control. Belle's breath hitched and she did it again. He hissed, his gaze meeting hers once more.

She licked her lips and, their hands still entwined, raised one his to scrape her teeth along his knuckles, to run her tongue over his palm.

Mitch exploded. His guttural cry of pleasure set hers free. Belle felt the power of his climax, her own body shuddered with wave after wave of the most incredible sensations.

Panting, she dropped onto his chest. Mitch's arms wrapped around her in a hug that was more emotional than sexual and brought tears to Belle's eyes. Just orgasm overload, she assured herself as she struggled to catch her breath.

"Now aren't you sorry you didn't take me up on my offer earlier?" she teased, trying to lighten the mood.

"Better late than never," he said with a laugh, his own breath sounding labored. "And keep in mind, I only get better with age."

Didn't that image simply boggle the mind? Belle shifted her legs so they lay alongside Mitch and hummed at the mini climax she felt at the move.

"Tell you what, gorgeous. If you only improve with age, you're going to be off the charts by the time you're forty."

Mitch snickered but Belle fell silent, realizing she wouldn't know. She'd be nowhere around in eight years when Mitch hit that milestone. Some other woman would likely be reaping the rewards of his age-improved sexual games. But not Belle. She'd thrown away—or rather, run away from—the right to know.

The idea made her miserable. Her stomach pitched and her eyes filled. Blaming it on emotional overload brought on by four orgasms in a row, Belle sniffed and rolled away to hide her tears. What now? Did she pat him on the ass, hand him his jeans and get back to business? It sounded so cold when all she wanted was to curl up in his arms and be held.

"Getting that good takes a lot of practice," Mitch mused, wrapping his arms around her from behind and tugging her back against his hot, naked body. "I have a few ideas I've wanted to try out on you, with you."

The painful tension eased from Belle's body, only to be replaced by tension of the sexual kind. Much happier with horny over weepy, she turned in Mitch's arms and grinned. "Do tell. I'm always intrigued by self-improvement programs."

He laughed and in a single move stood and scooped her up in his arms. Belle linked her hands behind his head and cuddled, a soft glow of joy settling in her chest.

"We need a mattress for what I have in mind," he told her, heading for the bedroom. "Something soft and comfortable, since next time I want you on the bottom."

"Sounds prosaic," she teased as he dropped her on the bed.

"Prosaic, my ass," he growled, kneeling at the bottom of the bed to take hold of her foot, still shod in her strappy sandal. A few quick flicks of his fingers and he'd unstrapped first one, then the other. Sliding his hands up her body in a way that left yummy tingles, he reached her mouth and planted a quick, hard kiss on her lips.

Before Belle could respond, he rolled away and shot a swift glance around the room. Her open closet apparently offered exactly what he was looking for, because he leaped from the bed and grabbed two belts and a silk scarf.

Belle's jaw dropped when he grabbed her wrist and, using a soft suede belt, tied it to the headboard.

"You're kidding," she breathed, scared, intrigued and totally turned on, all at the same time.

He didn't answer, instead holding out his hand and waiting. With a silent gulp, her breath coming a little faster as her body heated, Belle put the fingers of her free hand in his. Mitch tied it to the headboard as well, then lay on the bed next to her.

His gaze moved over her captive body like a caress. Her nipples peaked at his look, damp heat pooling between her legs. He stared for so long, she started to squirm.

Meeting her gaze, Mitch's eyes were hot and intense, filled with sexual promises. Belle pressed her lips together to keep from whimpering.

"I've wanted to tie you up for what feels like forever," he said softly. "Keep you here, at my mercy where you can't run or hide. Now that I have you, I'm going to touch you, kiss you, taste you." He ran the length of silk fabric between his fingers, then trailed it along her hip, over her quivering belly, and draped it gently over her aching breasts. "I'm going to use my tongue and my fingers. I'm going to drive you crazy."

Then he shifted, pulling the fabric from her breasts so the silky texture teased her nipples. Belle gasped and pressed her thighs together to ease the building pressure.

"And I'm going to do it all while you're blindfolded," he told her. Belle's gasp was lost in his mouth as he kissed her senseless while wrapping the jade-green silk over her eyes and tying it gently behind her head.

Belle planted her bare feet on the mattress, raising her pelvis in supplication. Mitch moved so he was between her wide-spread legs, his hard dick brushing against her aching center, but not relieving any tension, not entering her. She felt him lean forward, the mattress dipping on either side of her as he supported himself.

Holding her breath, she waited. Damp and hot, his tongue licked one nipple, then the other. A gentle gust of air teased the already hard peaks into aching stiffness. Belle couldn't hold back her whimper now. She needed something, anything.

"Do me," she begged.

"My way."

His way was killing her.

Still keeping that delicious pressure against her clit, he shifted. His hands cupped her breasts, pressing them together, his thumbs working her nipples as his mouth worked them in turn. Sucking, nibbling, licking. Teeth and tongue, just rough enough to make her crazy with need.

Oh, man. She was going to come before he even reached her aching center. She just knew it. And, she realized as the orgasm exploded behind her eyes, she just loved it.

Later, much, *much* later, wrapped in plush towels warmed by the heated towel-bar, Belle and Mitch fell to her bed in a state of exhausted pleasure. Her eyelids drooping, she glanced at the clock and yawned. Five hours ago, they'd stopped off here so she could change her clothes for the tour.

And now she was floating on a cloud of sensual satisfaction like nothing she'd ever felt before. A tiny frown, all she had the energy for, creased her brow. If she hadn't messed up, she could have been floating like this for years. At least a few, she told herself, knowing the trophy-bride role wouldn't have worked for long.

Her thoughts ran like a snag in a favorite sweater, irritating and ugly, ruining her mood. If she'd been a trophy then, what was she now? Why was Mitch with her? Sudden lust? Tension seeped down her spine. What if she fell for him again? It'd hurt badly enough before, when she'd known it was only infatuation. What if this time, now that they'd had the incredible sex and she was able to deal with him on a one-on-one adult level, she really fell hard? What if he broke her heart?

Panic tightened the muscles across her back, her breath starting to hitch.

Mitch's hand curved around her waist, pulling her closer. His warm breath on her back was all it took to melt the icy fear. Determined not to ruin what had been the best sex of her life, she shoved her fears aside and let her mind empty.

"We missed exploring the grounds," she murmured sleepily.

Ever the gentleman, Mitch tugged the blankets over them before curling up behind her and draping one arm around her waist.

"Tomorrow," he said, his voice sounding as worn out as she felt.

Tomorrow. They had tomorrow. Belle drifted off to sleep, the satisfied smile on her face due more to that promise than the fact that she'd just had the most incredible sex of her life.

8

_____

"It was…incredible. Totally amazing," Belle rhapsodized over the phone. Her mind was still filled with the memory of her and Mitch, naked. Two hours had passed since he'd left her bed after a hot bout of early-morning delight and she could still taste him. She shifted, just a little, and her unused-to-such-wild-sex body felt the reminder of him inside her.

"But, I don't get it—when I'm with Mitch, I totally lose control," she admitted to her best friend from the very bed where she'd had that wild sex. Now, though, it was man-less as she carefully applied a second coat of blushing burgundy to her toenails.

"Well, good sex will do that to a gal. I thought you'd have realized that by now," Sierra returned grumpily. Belle felt a surge of guilt at the worry she was causing her partner.

Not enough to drop the subject, though.

"Ha-ha," Belle deadpanned, capping the polish and setting it on the bedside table. "I mean, I keep…" She trailed off, needing to talk about it but realizing how stupid she'd sound.

"Keep what? Having premature orgasms? Screaming in ecstasy loud enough to bring the gardeners running? Welcoming your climax with a litany of filthy porn words?"

Belle's jaw dropped. Not at the words, but at the tart tone. She pulled the phone away from her ear to stare at it in shock, then flipped over on the bed so she lay on her stomach.

"Something's wrong," she decided aloud. "Is there a problem with Eventfully Yours? Are you okay? What's going on?"

Silence. Then she actually heard Sierra shrug, the fabric of whatever she was wearing brushing against the phone. "No problems. Nothing's going on. Company is fine."

Shorthand for Sierra didn't want to talk about it.

One of the cornerstones of their lifelong friendship was knowing when to push the other and when to back off and let her stew. Belle's telltale clue to leave Sierra alone had always been how many millimeters her lower lip stuck out. A champion pouter, Sierra was open to commiserating if she had the lip out. But if she'd sucked it in, concentration-style, she was off-limits.

Belle silently cursed the distance between them and tried to figure out what to do.

"What lipstick are you wearing?" she asked.

"What kind of question is that?" When Belle didn't say anything, Sierra admitted, "I'm not wearing any right now."

Chewed it all off. Definitely off-limits. Automatically backing away from the confrontation, Belle shifted back to the original topic. "I feel like an idiot," she admitted, "but I keep losing my temper with Mitch. You know me, I don't get angry. This is so bizarre."

"You do, too, get angry," Sierra pointed out. "You just don't allow yourself to express it. You'll end up with ulcers if you don't learn to let go of some of that, you know."

"Apparently I've found my release valve."

"Sex'll work every time," her partner agreed. "But since I'm not getting any, I'd rather talk about something else, okay?"

Sierra would never be in danger of ulcers. Despite her unwillingness to share whatever was bothering her, she never bottled up her emotions. Why bother, she usually said, when it was so much more fun to let them spew all over like a well-shaken bottle of soda.

Except now, when she seemed to be holding them in even better than Belle ever had.

"Okay, so, um, did you get my notes about the sex-themed ideas?" Belle asked, obediently changing the topic. "I'm going to need additional staff to help set up for the pre-events. I think Mitch said something about his security team running checks on everyone to guarantee a complete media blackout."

"We've got two dozen independent contractors on file who've passed top security screenings. That should be enough, shouldn't it?"

Belle glanced at her leather portfolio, flipping pages with the pad of her finger so as not to smudge her fresh polish. "That should work, in addition to Lakeside's serving staff."

The two of them went over details for the upcoming opening, plus ideas for possible follow-up contracts, such as holiday-themed sex and weddings à la kink.

"I talked to a couple of bigwigs when I was handling the CEO gig last week," Sierra said after they'd wound up business. "You know, just a few questions about who they think the top developers are, what they'd do in today's real estate climate and economy, that kind of chit-chatty thing."

Belle sat up and drew her knees to her chest. She glanced at the tab in her notebook titled Dad and grimaced. She'd been so busy getting mad at, then getting on top of Mitch, she'd forgotten the most important reason she was here.

"And?"

"Things just suck right now. They all said the same thing your dad did. It's not the time to build. In their opinion, anyone sitting on a big fat piece of land is stuck with it for the next little while."

"The next little while will bankrupt Daddy."

Sierra gave a sympathetic sigh. "I know."

Out of the blue, Belle thought back to the contract she'd seen on Diana's desk. There was a luxury spa in the resort lobby— fancy and very upscale. And oddly enough, it was not owned by the hotel but was leasing the space from Lakeside. Was that an option for her dad's hotels? An additional income? It was worth looking into.

"Let me talk to a couple of people," she told Sierra. "I thought of something earlier, but I need to get some details to figure out if it even makes sense."

Belle stared out the window at the gorgeous golf course. Morning sun washed it in gentle light. Lush, green and exclusive. Her father's hotels were lovely, but not in the same category as Lakeside. This resort would cater to an elite clientele, whereas Forsham's catered to upscale business travelers, wedding parties and couples looking for indulgent getaways.

Maybe the spa angle was the answer to increasing the cash flow until the real estate market turned around and her father could sell the properties without losing everything. She watched the gardeners putter along the green in a golf cart, stopping every ten feet or so to check on the bizarre gopher population explosion, and sighed.

"I'm going to dinner with Mitch tonight," she said. "I'll see if I can get some hypothetical advice or something."

Sierra made a sound that could be taken as agreement, then said, "Just be sure you ask him before you throw your next fit."

"What? Why would I throw a fit?"

"I thought temper tantrums were your new foreplay."

"Ha." Belle started to laugh as she hung up, then stopped. What if he was only interested in her when she was pissy? Did he only want her because she was a challenge now? Unlike before when she'd tried to serve herself up on a platter?

She told herself she was being silly. But still, her initial reaction was to pick a fight as soon as she saw him. That wasn't fair, though. She had to know. Which meant she'd be an absolute doll all night, flirt to her heart's content with nary a hint of anger or confrontation, and see how it went.

Hell, no, she wasn't going to take the easy way out. Belle gathered all the confidence she could and squared her shoulders. She'd have him begging for sex again and she'd do it with a smile on her face.

"Reece?" Mitch frowned as he crossed the lobby to greet the tall guy in the cowboy hat. "What're you doing here?"

Unselfconsciously, he gave Reece a quick man-hug, the arm-around-the-shoulder kind that he knew wouldn't embarrass his ex–Green Beret cousin.

"I thought I'd drop in, check the place out," Reece said in his slow drawl.

"Check up on your investment, you mean?" Mitch asked, referring to the fact that all the family members were stockholders on the MC board of directors.

"Nah, just wanted to see what kind of trouble your sorry ass has been getting up to." Reece made a show of looking around. Mitch followed his gaze, taking in the towering potted plants, the glossy marble-inlaid floor and ornate rosewood check-in desk. Reece gave a nod. "Long way from home, cuz."

"Ain't that the truth." Mitch pulled back his shoulders and grinned with pride. "You think the whole family will turn out for the grand opening blowout event?"

Reece pulled a face and gave a slow shrug. "Not so sure about that. I mean, if I read your reports right, you're shifting focus from a ritzy resort to a sexually charged amusement park for the rich and famous. Might be a little racy for Grammy Lynn, if ya know what I mean."

Mitch snickered. "Grammy Lynn sent me a list of suggestions to make sure we were offering enough sexy options."

"I shoulda known." Like everything else about him, Reece's grin was slow and easy. That smile deceived the enemy into thinking he was slow, women into thinking he was easy. They soon found out they were wrong. He was also loyal, tenacious and brilliant, but few people outside the family knew that, since Reece had a habit of keeping everyone at arm's length.

Mitch stood visiting with his cousin, feeling on top of the world. Family, success and hot sex. What more could a man want? The image of Belle as he'd last seen her, naked except for a very satisfied smile, flashed through his mind. Mitch shoved it right back out, figuring a hard-on while discussing the resort's sex themes might give the wrong message. Besides, he was still trying to sort through how he felt about last night. Awesome sex aside—and damned if it hadn't been the most awesome of his life—his mind was a mess. He ricocheted between sexual satisfaction, concern over being led around by his dick, and terror that it'd meant nothing to her. Hell, he felt like a teenage girl PMSing.

For the twentieth time since leaving Belle that morning, Mitch shoved the worries aside and forced himself to focus on the here and now.

So he asked about Reece's business. His cousin had opened a security firm after leaving the service. While he consulted and supervised security for MC Development, there was definitely not enough business in Mitch's little world to keep a man like Reece busy. Instead he kept his wits sharp working as a for-hire body-guard, defense trainer and, as Mitch liked to rib him, all-round spy.

"Seriously," he asked when he'd been brought up to date on everything, "what're you doing out here? You didn't say anything about a visit when we talked the other day."

"I had some stuff to go over with you, wanted to take a look around. Maybe meet your planner and discuss the security list you sent on her behalf."

Well, shit. Mitch hummed. He'd known his family would have questions once they found out Belle was his new planner, but he'd figured he had plenty of time to come up with a reasonable explanation. And more important, plenty of time to get used to—and over—the wild sexual intensity that flamed between them before he was faced with the threat of it being extinguished by the past.

Maybe he could keep Reece and Belle apart? Tell her he'd meet her later, have Larry haul his cousin around for a tour?

Keeping his smile in place, Mitch felt his mind race with possibilities. Despite the mind games he was playing with himself, things were going too well right now. He wasn't ready to give this pleasure up. He'd dreamed of being with Belle for years, wanted her for what felt like forever. Bottom line, he wasn't letting reality—in any form—intrude on this time with her.

Not even his cousin.

BELLE WALKED out of the spa into the resort's lobby, a satisfied smile on her face and three pages of notes in her portfolio. Apparently, MC Development rented space to all the little boutiques in the resort. Which not only cut back on their overhead, but brought in a tidy little income as well.

With a purr of pleasure, she raised her hand to her nose and sniffed the rich, floral fragrance on her silky smooth skin. Smelled good, felt great. The owner, Kiki, was a savvy businesswoman with an eye for success.

Belle had a feeling they'd get along great, and she'd know for sure the next day when they had lunch together. That was enough time to run her idea past Sierra, work up an outline and make a quick phone call to Daddy.

And, she thought as she spied Mitch across the lobby, even more important, time for that couples' massage and chocolate bath she'd talked the spa owner into booking for them, despite the spa not being open yet.

With that in mind, she sauntered toward Mitch, her heels making a snappy sound as she crossed the marble floor. She focused on his jean-encased butt, so sweet and tempting, and wondered how long it'd be before she could bite it. Again.

For now, she settled on a pat when she reached him. "How'd you like to get naked and play in chocolate?" she asked, coming up behind him.

Mitch spun around, a look of appalled bewilderment on his face. Quick as lightning, he grabbed her hand off his ass and, with a gentle squeeze, shook it as if they were distant business acquaintances.

Hurt and confused, Belle tried to figure out what his problem was.

The sound of male laughter clued her in. She glanced around Mitch's shoulder and saw a lanky, Southern hunk seated on the white-leather couch and realized she'd embarrassed Mitch. At least she hoped that look had been embarrassment and not distaste for her suggestion.

Putting on her best society-princess smile, she stepped around Mitch and held out her hand in greeting. As the guy got to his feet, she gave a mental frown and tried to place him. He looked vaguely familiar.

"I'm Belle Forsham, and I'm afraid I've reached my limit of naughty offers for the day, but I hope we can be friends anyway?" she greeted in a light, joking tone.

"Reece Carter. It's a pleasure to meet you." It wasn't the touch of his large hand engulfing hers that clued Belle in. It was Mitch's supportive one grazing the small of her back. "Again."

A buzzing rang in Belle's ears, and her breath stuck somewhere in her chest. Carter. Mitch's cousin. The cousin, she remembered, that Mitch considered his best friend and had asked to be his best man. That's why he looked so familiar. He'd attended their kyboshed wedding and probably thought, with good reason, that she was a flaky bitch from hell.

Gathering what little nerve she had and taking strength from Mitch's warmth, she looked into Reece's midnight-blue eyes, but she saw no trace of judgment. Just an odd sort of waiting. The steady gaze made her stomach hurt. Maybe censure would have been better?

Mitch's cell phone rang and he excused himself, stepping away to take the call. She didn't know why, but Belle wanted to grab his belt loop and follow him to safety.

She offered Reece a hesitant smile. He didn't return it. Instead he gave her a long, intimidating stare that let her know without words that yes, he definitely remembered what she'd done and flaky bitch from hell was the nicest way he could think of her.

Belle wondered how fast she could run in these heels.

"I hear your naughty suggestions are going to be the highlight of this resort," Reece finally said.

Oh, fun, talking sex with a guy who completely hated her. She'd rather take her chances with her heels, but for Mitch's sake, she knew she couldn't.

Belle swallowed twice, trying to wet her tongue. She stretched her lips into a smile. "They'll make Lakeside the go-to playground of the rich and famous. I'm not sure how much Mitch has shared, but we have some great ideas that I know will lay a solid promotional foundation."

Realizing she was babbling, Belle stopped and pressed her lips together. She barely heard Mitch rejoin them and take over the description of their plans for the resort. She wanted, no needed, to leave. Now.

"Gentlemen, I'm so sorry, but I have to run," she interrupted.

Mitch frowned at her. "I thought we were having lunch." He looked at his watch, then gestured to his cousin. "Reece'll join us. We can go now if you're hungry."

She'd really been looking forward to eating with Mitch. Lunch and a little footsie, some flirting and maybe a quickie nooner for dessert.

"Um, I can't. I'm sorry, but I forgot I need to run by your office and talk to Diana about a few things. I need to use her fax to send off some contracts, too."

Belle knew she was a rotten liar and now apparently so did the men standing in front of her. Mitch gave her an angry look that slowly shifted to suspicion, staring at her as if she was an intriguing puzzle with a few vital pieces missing.

"We'll do dinner instead, then," he said after a few moments. He used his business voice. The one that let her know he was speaking as the guy signing her contract, not the guy who'd done her doggy-style before breakfast.

"I'll look forward to it," she lied before turning to make her way across the marble foyer toward the questionable refuge of Mitch's office. It had been a stupid lie, since the men could easily and justifiably follow her, but her brain had stalled. When she saw them head toward the restaurant, she heaved a sigh of relief.

Not willing to be proved the liar she was, she decided to go visit Diana anyway. Just CYA.

She scurried down the hallway and into Mitch's assistant's office. Except Diana wasn't there. Belle gave a huff of frustration and debated her options. She could just go to her cottage, but that meant losing her witness. She could wait for Diana, but, well, she really didn't like the gal enough to waste who knew how long twiddling her thumbs.

Or, she eyed the fax machine, she could send a fax as she'd said she would. That would turn her lie into a truth and make it all right. She grinned at her twisted justification and, flipping open her portfolio, grabbed the specs from the spa and penned a quick note to Sierra to outline her idea. She'd planned to e-mail them all, but hey, faxing meant she didn't have to type up all the specs since she didn't have a scanner.

She rolled her eyes at the continual justification.

"Hey, Belle."

She turned and saw Larry in the doorway and grinned. Perfect. "Hey, Larry, how's it going?"

"I'm glad I found you. I pitched an idea to Mitch about bringing in a live band each month and he said to get together with you to expand on it."

They chit-chatted as she set her stuff on the armoire housing the office equipment and slid her papers into the fax machine's paper feed. Punching in Eventfully Yours's number, she listened to the manager's ideas and considered tasteful ways to integrate the sex themes.

Before she could offer any feedback, Larry glanced at his watch and shrugged. "Lunch over, I've gotta run. I'll send you a memo about this, okay?"

She nodded and said goodbye as she gathered the faxed papers from the tray.

Well, that had worked out nicely. Despite being bummed at being cheated out of her lunchtime sexual romp, and very nervous over the arrival of Mitch's cousin, Belle was feeling pretty good as she sorted the specs to put back in her portfolio.

As she filed them, she noticed a crumpled ball of paper stuck under the fax tray. She tugged the wad out and, about to toss it in the trash, noticed the word *gopher.* Had Mitch found a way to get rid of the pests? She smoothed the page flat and glanced at it. A memo typed on Lakeside's stationery.

Then she read it from beginning to end.

Confused, she turned it over, looking for what she didn't know.

Was someone deliberately causing damage to Mitch's resort? She looked at the typed to-do list.

Damage sprinklers, reroute laundry, break bench slats. The list went on and on. Brow furrowed, a sick feeling in her stomach, she scanned the rest. And right there, gophers on the golf course.

She bit her lip and wondered briefly where the hell one imported gophers from, then shook her head. Did it matter? Someone was doing all of this deliberately. Messing with Mitch's property, trying to screw up or ruin the launch of the resort. She flipped to the second page and noticed a handwritten note. Her stomach sank as her vision wavered in shock.

Keep up the good work. This is exactly what Mitch asked for. Inflict as much damage as possible before the end of the month.

It was signed with the initials L.N.

"YOU DIDN'T mention your event planner was the little blonde who turned your world upside down a few years back."

"Belle?" Mitch grimaced and took a drink of his coffee to buy time. "I sent the specs on Eventfully Yours. I'm sure you read her qualifications."

"Glowing. And nary a mention that she'd once planned the event that left you doing a solo act at the altar." Typically, Reece's voice held no judgment. Just a musing sort of curiosity.

"She's the best planner on the west coast. Her company is perfect for what I want here, and she's already proved her worth by coming up with the theme idea that you yourself claimed was brilliant," Mitch defended. When Reece just stared, Mitch rolled his eyes and shrugged. "Let's face it, she was right to call it quits six years ago. Getting married was insane. I was the one in the wrong, marrying her to seal that deal with old man Forsham."

And to prove to everyone, including himself, that he was enough of a hotshot to score the boss's princess daughter. Mitch might admit that to himself, but he wasn't about to tell his cousin. Not that, nor the fact that he'd straight up used Belle's desire, their sexual attraction for each other to manipulate her into the engagement.

"You trust her?" was all Reece said.

Mitch shrugged. "In business, sure." In bed, too. "I'd think twice if it involved rings or ministers though."

Their waiter arrived with lunch and both men fell silent.

Hoping the topic was over, Mitch picked up his knife and fork and cut into his Baja grilled chicken. Reece lifted his Angus burger, but before taking a bite he gestured with it and claimed, "Your girl's nervous about something. Might be the past. Might be more. I'm going to do a little checking."

"Don't bother," Mitch said, his brow furrowing. "I trust Belle, okay?"

"Glad to hear it. Trust always makes the sex hotter, I'm sure." Reece's grin was quick, wicked and knowing. "But someone's deliberately screwing with you and this resort, cuz. And I find it mighty curious that you're having all these unexplained problems right about the same time your ex shows up. Can't hurt to poke around."

All Mitch heard was *deliberately.*

"You're sure it's sabotage?" he asked, all defensiveness over his past mistakes forgotten.

"Looks like."

"Check everyone." Fury flashed like a strobe light behind Mitch's eyes. *Deliberately.* He'd worked his ass off to get this far and someone was trying to ruin him. He clenched his fist, anger burning in his gut. He'd be damned if they'd get away with it. "I want whoever is behind this caught and strung up."

"And if it's the pretty blonde?"

Frowning, Mitch thought of Belle. Her smile, the laughter and fun she had teasing him. Mr. Winkles and the vulnerability she tried so hard to hide. The sexy way she walked across the room and the mewling sound she made when she came.

"It's not her," he declared, trying to shrug off the idea. "But before you tell me it's your job to check everyone thoroughly, I'm saying go ahead. Just don't be surprised to find out you're wrong."

Worry pounded at his temples until Mitch forced himself to think the situation through. Once he did, he was able to relax a little. After all, Belle might be a lot of things. A little flaky, impulsive and quick to react without thinking. Sexy, flirtatious and sweet, definitely. But the one thing he was positive about was that she wasn't a liar.

9

"YOU STILL haven't explained why we're here instead of your cottage." Mitch asked for the third time as he followed her down the short hall to one of the guest suites the next evening.

Belle glanced back at him, a thrill of excitement flashing at the sight of his version of evening casual. Jeans, a black button-up shirt and, her gaze dropped to his feet, dress shoes. He looked so good, even better now that she'd seen him naked. She sighed. The man was simply delicious.

And, she glanced at his face, so not the kind of guy who'd play some elaborate scam to screw over his own company. She'd asked him to trust her to make dinner arrangements, and had been gratified—and a little shocked—when he'd readily agreed. She figured this was the perfect time to do some subtle questioning, just to assure herself he was as innocent as she thought.

It had to be her own doubts that had her imagining the suspicion in his voice. Belle tried to shrug off the weird feeling, telling herself it was paranoia brought on by Reece's surprise arrival and the papers she'd found in Diana's office.

"It's a surprise," she told him again. With a deep breath, she reached into her purse to pull out the room card. Her tummy spun with nerves and she missed twice before she could get the flimsy card into the lock. She'd never been this nervous to present an event or theme to a client before.

Of course, she'd never planned to get the client naked before, either. She didn't know if it was that, or nerves over playing Mata Hari on a quest for secrets that made her feel so intimidated.

It definitely wasn't because they'd had the most intensely wild, passionate sex of her life or that it left her feeling emotionally naked and vulnerable. Worrying about that would be ridiculous, especially since she couldn't do anything about the vulnerability unless she was willing to stop having the incredible sex. And that was out of the question.

She told herself for at least the hundredth time since yesterday to quit obsessing. And while she was at it, just to put Reece-the-intimidating out of her mind and forget about the note and the suggestion that Mitch had asked for damage to be done to Lakeside. It just didn't make sense for him to ruin his own resort.

Belle shook her head as if she could knock the thoughts out of it. With a deep breath, she focused instead on the previous night, the great sex, and the hot lovin' she had planned for tonight. Whew, much better.

With a deep breath and a little wiggle of anticipation for what she hoped was about to come—namely her—Belle pushed open the heavy door.

"We're doing dinner here tonight," she said as she entered the dimly lit room. Hurrying before Mitch could get a good look around, she grabbed the lighter and lit the bank of candles on the dresser. "I thought we'd have a preview of what your guests can expect when they stay."

"Really?" Excitement, curiosity and a hint of naughty pleasure were all packed into that one word.

His tone instantly settled her nerves. Belle pasted on a seductive smile and turned to face Mitch. Leaning one hip on the dresser, she gestured to the room.

"What you see before you is a typical, luxurious resort suite. Comfortable seating, antique furnishings, good art. Quality all the way, which your guests will expect." She tilted her head toward the table in the corner, set up to her specifications. "A delicious private dinner for two, wine and a decadent and one-of-a-kind dessert. Yummy by any standard, but we're hinting at something more. Something, dare I say it, sexy?"

Mitch's lips twitched but he kept his expression intrigued instead of amused. "Sexy?"

"Just a hint," she demurred, stepping to the table and curving her fingers around the handles of the domed silver covers she'd instructed the kitchen to find. She wanted that movie-star ambiance. Lifting the covers, she set them aside and gestured again, this time toward the loveseat next to the table.

Oysters, asparagus, lobster and a spice-encrusted steak. This time Mitch didn't bother to hide his grin. Instead he stepped forward, and after a quick glance at the table pulled her into his arms for a kiss that put the ninety-dollar-a-plate meal behind them to shame.

Belle gave herself over to the kiss, needing it in a way she couldn't even explain to herself. Maybe because it was the first one since he'd left her curled up naked in her sheets, or maybe it was just the nerves, but as soon as his lips touched hers, her entire body relaxed in one huge sigh of relief. She was silly to suspect him.

A kiss and a grope later, Belle peeled her fingers off his ass and they settled on the plushly cushioned loveseat for their meal.

"This is fabulous," he said after a few bites of his steak. "Not just the private dinner, but the whole setup. The candlelight and roses, the view—" he gestured to the open balcony window and the moonlit copse of trees "—it all adds to the romantic ambiance."

Pleased, Belle glanced around the room. That worked perfectly with her theme. Romance went hand in hand with sexual fantasies.

But the theme would be pointless if whoever made that list hit their goal and Lakeside went belly-up before the end of the year. Belle squared her shoulders, remembering her private mission for the evening. Dig.

"So, how's it all coming for the resort's opening?" she asked as they ate. "It's just a week until the first party, three weeks until the doors open to the public. Is everything ready to go on your end?"

A tiny frown came and went, but Mitch just shrugged and nodded. "It's coming along. Things will move a little smoother now that Reece is here."

Was that because Reece was Mr. Security? Did Mitch know who was behind the problems and had brought his cousin out to catch them? Or was Reece here to stop any further incidents? For about the hundredth time, Belle considered showing Mitch the list. But, as always, she recalled the comment about the damage being something he'd requested and held back.

"You've run security checks on all the resort employees, haven't you? Including management?" That memo had definitely been sent by someone who wouldn't be questioned hanging out in Diana's office.

"Sure, a check is standard and we sent around those confidentiality agreements you wanted, too." The look he gave her, curious and just a little suspicious, let her know it was time to change the subject.

"Wait till you see dessert," Belle said, shifting so her thigh slid along his. The move pulled the hem of her dress higher, leaving bare thigh pressed to the rough fabric of his jeans. "Since I thought it'd be better to postpone the chocolate spa treatment until, um, later," like, after Reece had left, "I came up with a fun after-dinner treat that has a similar effect."

Tearing his eyes from her silky thigh and its hint of the

naked delight barely hidden by her dress, Mitch looked at her and frowned. "Chocolate spa treatment? What's that?"

"I met with your spa owner to discuss some ideas I had." Like finding out if Kiki, who was looking to launch two more spas, might want to consider renting space in a Forsham Hotel. But that wasn't her point. "She and I came up with a dozen or so sexy themed services she'll offer and I booked us to try the couples' chocolate spa treatment."

Belle had also noted that none of the "accidents" had affected the spa or any of the other privately owned businesses. Only Mitch's direct holdings.

"Sounds…intriguing," he said with a grin. Setting his fork down, Mitch rested his hand on her knee. His warm fingers sent a tingle of excitement up her bare thigh all the way to the heated core between her legs. She wanted to shift, to encourage him to slide his hand higher and discover for himself that she was commando under her slinky black dress. But she was on a mission. Besides, part of the fun was anticipation, so she forced herself to be still.

"Why'd you cancel the appointment?" he asked.

"I…" She'd been so distracted by Reece's appearance, and then her discovery that someone was deliberately trying to tank the resort, she'd forgotten to confirm a time. Belle tried to come up with a decent excuse, but his fingers were making a slow, hot trip north and she couldn't think straight. "Um, you have family here."

Mitch's jaw dropped. Belle frowned. She didn't so much mind shocking him, but she did mind that his fingers stopped their delicious journey.

"What?" she asked when he started laughing, not sure why she felt so self-conscious all of a sudden. It wasn't as though she'd confessed that she'd spent months practicing her signature as Mrs. Belle Carter.

"I'm just surprised," he admitted. "I mean, I would have sworn you didn't have a shy bone in your body."

"I don't," Belle snapped, offended.

"And yet now that we're not having anonymous, hotel-employees-are-totally-discreet sex, you're taking it into hiding?"

"Did you want to ask your cousin to come watch?" Belle shot back without thinking. "Or maybe videotape us doing it in the shower to show at the next family reunion?"

"Most of the family will be here for the pre-event next week," Mitch mused. "We can show it then. Really kick off this sex theme with a big bang."

She stared in slack-jawed shock, irritated embarrassment forgotten.

"You'd actually show your family sex tapes?" She couldn't even read romance novels in the presence of her father, he was so uptight about the topic.

"Nah, I was teasing. They don't want to see my naked butt move to some porn soundtrack." Mitch grinned and gave a rueful shake of his head. "But they are amazing, especially my grandma. She pretty much raised all my cousins and me."

"And your sister?" Remembering Mitch's snotty sister from their abandoned wedding, Belle hid her grimace in a fake smile. She'd spent months regretting not letting Sierra kick her rude ass.

"Sister?" He frowned, then his face cleared and he shook his head again. "Lena? We lived in the same house for a year or so when my mom first married her dad, but then she left for college. After our parents died, we grew apart. We reconnected right before I went to work for your dad. I'd decided to merge her late father John's construction company with MC Development and I needed her signature."

Belle remembered the bland woman's taunts as if it were yesterday. Of course, she'd replayed her "runaway" reel in her head a million times, so that actually felt like yesterday, too. Lena had been so cocky about her knowledge of Mitch's character.

"Most of my family is on the board of MC Development, except her. I offered her a chair, but she had other things going on. Other than Lena, who never really hung out much, the family is really tight. When I was growing up, my grandma was the family babysitter. Even after she remarried, my mom was a working woman. All my aunts were, too."

The love he had for his family was clear in his voice. Belle felt a twinge of jealousy. Sure, she loved her dad, but they weren't tight like Mitch's family seemed to be. Would she have been welcomed in if they'd gotten married? The thought of what she might have had made her want to cry, so she gestured to Mitch to keep talking.

"The family all lived within four blocks of each other so instead of after-school care, my cousins and I went to Gram's house." Mitch went on to describe his childhood and random details about what various cousins and family members were doing now. From the sound of it, each and every one would be arriving at the resort the following week.

Belle felt like throwing up her perfectly delicious lobster. All of them. Here. Knowing exactly what she'd done to Mitch, how she'd run away on their wedding day. Wouldn't parading naked down Rodeo Drive be easier?

"So that's why you cancelled the chocolate and sex massage?" Mitch asked as he finished the last of his dinner. "Because you didn't want my cousin to know we're practicing what you preach?"

Embarrassed heat washed over Belle from the top of her forehead to the edge of her bra. She hated when she blushed. The color totally clashed with her hair.

Trying to save face, she just shrugged and pointed out, "This is what your clientele would be dealing with, you know? They want to have wild, uncensored sex and the oddest things cause inhibition. You might want to talk to your cousin about making sure the resort's security is solid. That'll be crucial if you want to pull this off."

Mitch's arched brow told her he hadn't missed her blatant avoidance of an answer, but he let it pass. "I've set up a meeting between you and Reece for tomorrow," he said.

Belle licked her lips. Meet with Reece? Alone? Um, no. Even though he'd been perfectly cordial through dinner the previous evening, she hadn't forgotten that threatening look he'd given her when they'd first met. He obviously had it in for her, and while he might be willing to play nice in front of his cousin, she had no doubt the gloves would come off in private.

"Can we make it the day after?" she asked, buying time as she stood and made her way over to the second room in the suite. Time for dessert. Or at least a change of topic.

Mitch just shrugged in answer. His attention, she realized, was on the bedroom. The bedroom containing her pièce de résistance, the culmination of her sex-themed evening. Her nerves returned. Fingers laced together, she tried to keep herself from bouncing in her high heels as she waited for his reaction.

MITCH FELT like he'd died and gone to heaven. A delicious dinner, Belle, and from the look of the bedroom and glimpse of the bath he could see from the doorway, a very hot night yet to come.

Like the romantic dinner, the dimly lit bedroom screamed romance. A midnight-red trail of rose petals lay strewn over the floor and across the cool, white expanse of the turned-down bed. Every surface held candles waiting to be lit. He squinted, trying to see the array of items displayed on the silver tray on the nightstand. The thick, knobby curve on one of the things worried him a little. Belle had talked about sex toys for the guests, but he wasn't sure he was ready to play hide the dildo with her. The light glanced off something metal—handcuffs, he realized. He'd just have to cuff her to the bed before she hauled out the Rabbit vibrator.

He glanced at Belle, who was trying to read his reaction. The moonlight shone through the window, casting a glow of pearls over her skin and blond hair, tousled and sexy for their date. But the luminescent beauty that tugged at his heart was all hers.

She nibbled her sweet lower lip between her teeth, brows raised in question. Mitch could see the nerves in her sea-green eyes, that underlying worry he'd been so surprised to find in such a confident woman. He supposed that was why she was so good at what she did. She cared, really cared about her clients loving her work.

Not that he saw this as being about business, of course. What was between them was all personal. No matter how she tried to wrap it up as justifying her contract. Or how much Reece tried to argue that Belle was only after some weird revenge by sabotaging his resort.

"I take it this is phase two of our evening?" he asked.

"The dessert phase," she responded seriously.

Mitch glanced around again, but didn't see anything resembling food. "I take it we're each other's treat?"

Which suited him perfectly. Feasting on the sweetness of Belle's body was an ideal ending to a delicious dinner.

Her eyes danced in delight as she giggled, but Belle shook her head. "No, no. I wouldn't cheat you out of a yummy ending to such a special dinner. Dessert is waiting."

Mitch followed her gesture toward the bathroom, then glanced back at her in question. Hardly his idea of the ideal eating place.

"I need a couple of minutes to get everything ready," she said, sounding a little breathless. He hoped it was anticipation and not amusement. "While I'm preparing the surprise, why don't you think about preparing yourself for a little fun?"

He looked over at the dildo, even bigger now that he could see it clearly, and arched his brow. She followed his gaze and laughed aloud. "No, no, that's just a sampling for the guests. You don't want to judge what they might indulge in. You just want to give them plenty to choose from."

"And your choice is?"

"You," she said, the laughter fading as she stepped close and pressed her hands against his chest. He automatically reached up to curve his fingers over her breasts so lovingly encased in filmy black fabric. Her nipples perked under his palms, her breath hitched just a little as she stepped up on tiptoe to meet his lips.

Mitch tasted the rich lobster, butter and the sweetness that was all Belle as he sank into the kiss. Tongues danced a slow, wicked waltz, making him painfully aware that the bed was waiting just a few feet away.

Needing more, he curved one hand behind her neck and felt the hooks that held her halter dress together. With a flick of his fingers, the fabric loosened and skimmed down her body.

"We'll call this a taste of what's to come," she purred with a satisfied look on her face. Belle stepped away, wearing nothing but a strappy pair of black sandals and gorgeous smile. "While I get the next course ready, why don't you undress? I hate to be the only naked body enjoying the treat."

Screw the treat. Mitch wanted her. Now. He reached out to grab her but Belle danced away, surprisingly nimble in such high spiked heels.

"No, not yet. Go undress." She gave a little wave of her fingers toward the other side of the room. "I want to do this for you, okay? For you, with you. You'll love it."

With that and the mouthwatering view of her naked ass as she scurried from the room, she was gone.

Mitch sighed and, after a quick recitation of the first twenty

U.S. presidents, managed to return the blood from his throbbing dick back to his brain.

Deciding she was right and naked would get him inside her hot, wet body sooner, he stripped. From the bathroom and dressing area he heard the rush of water in the tub, the clinking of glass and, at one excruciating point, her moan of delight.

"She'd better not be starting without me," he muttered as he left his jeans in a pile with the rest of his clothes.

Naked and rock-hard, Mitch strode across the room. When he reached the suite's dressing area, he noticed the carved, tufted rosewood dressing bench had been covered in thick towels. Next to it was a small glass table, a bowl and two spoons. The bowl was filled with what looked like ice cream and some kind of topping, making Mitch's mouth water as he thought about eating the treat off Belle's naked belly.

Steam poured from the open bathroom door, the scent of peaches and heat filling the room. Like a dream, Belle stepped out of the steam naked. Droplets of water dotted her bare flesh, one trailing a wet caress to the tip of her right breast.

Mesmerized, Mitch walked across the room, not breathing until he reached her. He bent down and sipped at her wet nipple, making her mewl like a kitten begging to be petted.

His hands moved easily over her damp skin, up and down the planes of her back twice before he pressed his fingers into the curve at the base of her spine to bring her tight against his body. His sips now turned to nibbles. One hand slid around her waist and down between their bodies to cup her damp and, he realized in shock, very bare sex.

Mitch pulled back from his feast to see the discovery his fingers had made.

"Well, well," he said with a grin.

Belle giggled, then arched one brow in a vampy look. "A smooth surface was better for what I have in mind."

"Later," he dismissed, wanting to run his fingers and tongue over that silky expanse of bare flesh.

"Uh-uh," she corrected, stepping back. "Keep your hand on your bird and not in my bush."

"A bird in the hand is worth two in a bush," he corrected absently, shooting her a grin. "Besides, you're bushless now."

Belle's giggle made Mitch feel like a million bucks. The simple fact that here she was, the princess of his dreams, naked, laughing and totally focused on him— Well, it blew his mind. Mitch recalled how excited he'd been to buy the resort, to see what he'd thought of as his dream actually come true.

But he looked at the woman staring up at him, amusement and happiness clear on her face, and realized this was his real dream come true.

"Come see why naked is better." Oblivious to the shocked realization that'd just kicked Mitch in the face, Belle grabbed his hand and pulled him back to the dressing area, where she'd set up the towel-covered settee and dessert.

Telling himself he'd overreacted and to focus on the naked woman and incredible sex in store for him, Mitch shoved aside the emotional bomb and watched Belle. His mouth watered both at the richly sweet scent filling the air and the sight of her naked ass as she swayed across the room, still wearing those sexy do-me heels.

Wiggling her brows at Mitch and giving him a look that was a combination of flirtation and amusement, Belle sat in demure nudity on the cushioned bench. She lifted a crystal bowl filled with ice cream, peaches and what looked like a caramel sauce.

"Freshly made vanilla-bean ice cream, brandied peaches and caramel," she told him as she held out the bowl for him to see. Then she puffed out her lip in an exaggerated pout and gave a tiny shrug. "But it's so rude to eat out of the serving bowl, isn't it? So you'll be my dessert plate and I'll eat off you, hmm?"

His cock jumped at the image of her eating dessert off his body and it was all Mitch could do not to grab the bowl and pour the sweet confection over himself.

"What about my dessert?" he asked, the gentlemanly part of him struggling to overcome the powerful urging of his dick.

"You'll get to eat all you want later," she promised. When he started to protest, she made a tut-tutting noise and shook her head. "Ladies first, remember."

He told himself it was manners that stifled his protest, but they both knew it was the fact that she took his hands and pulled him forward so his dick was level with her breasts.

Visions and ideas flashed through his head, each one more erotic than the last. But before he could act on any, Belle shook her head again and dropped to her knees so he was now level with her mouth. She lifted the bowl and with a wink she blew him a kiss and poured.

Mitch groaned at the sensation of cold ice cream and warm caramel sauce sliding over his straining head. Then Belle added her hot mouth to the mix. His hips bucked, and unable to help himself, Mitch tunneled his fingers through her hair and held on as she blew him and his control all to hell.

His orgasm hit hard, fast and intense, and Mitch growled with pleasure when Belle didn't stop sucking, licking or nibbling away at her dessert. Everything went black, his knees almost buckling as he gave over to the pleasure pumping out of his body.

It took him a solid minute to regain his senses. When he came back to earth, he realized Belle had stopped sucking and had laid her head against his belly and was giving him a hug, her arms wrapped around his thighs.

He smoothed a caress down the back of her tousled hair, causing Belle to pull back and grin up at him.

"Now that was a tasty dessert," she purred. "Shall we follow it up with a relaxing bath and wash off the stray peaches?"

"What about mine?" he asked, wanting nothing more than to taste her juices mixed with hot caramel.

"Help yourself," Belle said with a wink.

Mitch noted a peach stuck to her shoulder and grinned. He scooped it up with one finger and popped it into his mouth, then proceeded to enjoy the clean, smooth pleasure of peaches, Brazilian style.

Ten minutes later Mitch sighed with pleasure as he held her back against his chest and sipped champagne in the huge spa tub.

"So what do you think of this particular theme?" she asked, her face still flushed from her climax.

"It's perfect. Traditional yet just kinky enough to appeal to the average guest," he assured her. "Like everything else you've come up with, it's perfect."

"Wait till you see the setup for the kinkier guests. You know the ones—seen it all, done it all." He felt her laugh as her shoulders shifted against his chest. "The leather goods, floor-to-ceiling poles and edgier sex toys arrived this afternoon."

"I can't wait to try them out," he assured her before taking a drink. The explosion of bubbles, alcohol and peaches filled his taste buds and Mitch sighed. Damn, life was good.

"Hmm, I think that means I deserve a reward," she mused. Wicked humor lit her green eyes, but before she could take charge of their lovemaking again, Mitch set down the champagne flute and grabbed her hips.

A quick move and he had her pressed against the opposite side of the tub, her breasts just above water level and her butt up in the air.

His fingers went to work on her nipples as Mitch sucked and licked the trail of water up her spine until he reached the back of her neck.

His body holding her in place, he slipped into the glorious

wet pleasure of her body from behind. Belle's moan was breathy, lost in her soft pants of delight.

The steamy heat, the slickness of the water added another level of decadence to their lovemaking. Mitch took his time, building her pleasure with long, even strokes countered by tiny flicks of his fingers over her wet, turgid nipples.

When Belle couldn't handle it anymore, her pants becoming whimpers and her body pressing tighter against him, he pulled out, turned her in one swift move and pulled her right back down on his throbbing dick. The move, so hard and fast, sent him over the edge and his explosion of pleasure brought her right along. His mouth took hers as they came together. Belle's gasping cry of his name added an emotional edge to his orgasm.

He scooped her slippery slick body out of the frothy bubbles and, still kissing her, carried Belle into the other room. Uncaring that they soaked the sheets, he dropped to the bed, pulling her with him. He couldn't release his hold on her, not even to grab a towel, to pull up the blankets. He didn't want to let go of Belle.

Ever.

His last thought before sleep wound its way through his sexual haze was that he couldn't wait to introduce Belle to his grandma. Six years ago, he'd used the excuse of their rushed wedding as his reason for not bringing her into his family circle. The truth was, he'd been afraid of losing her.

This time, he knew it'd work out.

This time was forever.

10

"KNOCK IT OFF, Reece," Mitch snapped the next afternoon. His glare should have slain the man in his tracks, but his damned cousin was made of tougher stuff. "I don't want to hear this crap. It's bullshit, you're wasting my time."

"Cuz, I know you don't want to hear bad about your lady-friend, but you have to face facts. Someone is screwing you over and everything is pointing in her direction."

"Belle isn't behind the sabotage. It was happening long before she signed on. There's no reason to suspect her." He slammed his fist on his desk. Mitch's vision blurred as fury filled his brain. "What's your problem with her, Reece? Are you holding on to a grudge on my behalf? Do you hate blondes? Is Belle just too much for you? What exactly is the problem here?"

The fury did a slow burn as his cousin just sat there calmly, staring in silence. The contrast of his own anger and Reece's composure only added fuel to Mitch's frustration.

Then, stretching his jaw to either side, Reece pulled off his cowboy hat and contemplated the curve of the brim before setting it back on his head. Preparing for battle. Mitch recognized the move and steeled himself to win. Because there was no way in hell he was backing down.

"Look, I know you're into the gal and I'm not saying I have a personal issue with her." At Mitch's glare, Reece shrugged and admitted, "Well, other than the whole screwing-you-over-and-leaving-you-standing-there-with-your-dick-in-your-hand thing, I don't have a personal issue with her."

Mitch thought about defending his dick-holding practices as his business, but realized it'd be a waste of time. Family defended family, end of story.

"But you have to be realistic. Your resort is seeing problems and this gal has a history of problems. She also knows the hotel business inside out. She's the daughter of a guy who thinks you screwed him royally. And, well, bottom line, she's female."

Mitch squinted. "Care to justify that last one?"

"She's a woman. Women do the strangest things. Who knows, she might have spent the last half-dozen years stewing over whatever it was that pissed her off enough to leave you at the altar and is just now implementing her revenge."

The flames of his fury were doused as if they'd been hit by a deluge of water. Mitch just shook his head in pity. "You still reeling from your divorce, cuz?"

"Nah, I'm over the hangover now." Reece shot him a grin that Mitch had seen turn women from disinterested divas into panting groupies. Mitch was probably the only person who knew that grin was hiding a pained heart. Not broken, but bruised. Even Reece would be surprised at the news.

"Shawna aside, since she was in a class by herself, I just don't get what goes through their pretty little heads sometimes," Reece continued with a shrug.

Mitch didn't comment. There wasn't much to say since he'd never cared two damns about what went on in a woman's head until Belle had showed up—this time, he forced himself to acknowledge. Their first round, his only interest had been in proving himself, in snagging the biggest prize in the game.

"You said you wanted me to investigate." Reece's grin fell away as he leaned forward to rest his elbows on his knees. The look he speared Mitch with was all business. "That means man up and listen to the results of that investigation, regardless of what your dick wants to hear."

Mitch set his jaw and with a jerk of his head indicated his cousin offer up those results.

Reece stared for another few seconds, then lifted a file folder from the seat next to him. He held it up for Mitch to see, then without opening it tossed it on the desk.

"You've had a series of e-mails coming out of the resort. Not unusual," he said before Mitch could scoff, "except that each one is going to the same IP address and each one is deleted from your server. A few a week, sometimes more, never less."

Mitch frowned and laid his palm on the file.

"Interviewing the staff and repair crew involved in each incidence, I think it's clear the problems the resort's faced in the last month have all been deliberate. The lost linens, the destruction of property, even the gophers."

Mitch pulled his head back in shock. How the hell did someone come up with that many gophers?

"The gophers, by the way," Reece continued, pointing a finger at the file folder under Mitch's hand, "were actually shipped direct to the resort. Ballsy move, that."

Mitch pulled the folder toward him but didn't open it.

"From what I've gathered, the person behind it is a woman."

Mitch glared, but waited for the justification he knew was coming.

"I say that because all of the destruction was smallish, things easily broken by someone of a slight stature." He went on to list the items to support his supposition. While he listened, Mitch flipped open the file folder and scanned the reports of property damage. With each one, his anger and frustration mounted.

"You really think all that is definitive evidence it's a woman behind the problems?" Mitch asked, his tone dismissive. He had small guys on the crew and in his management team. He was sure it could have been any of them.

"Nah, that's all circumstantial." Reece leaned out of his chair and across the desk to flip the pages in Mitch's hand to a manifest. "That the gophers were delivered to and signed for by a woman is definitive."

Mitch stared at the loopy and decidedly feminine scrawl on the delivery manifest. Two dozen gophers, signed for by Janie Doe. He hated that his brain was scrambling to remember Belle's signature. He glanced at the date on the invoice. The same as the date of her first visit to talk him into hiring her. Mitch felt sick, but told himself it wasn't her. His gut knew it wasn't, but there weren't many women at the resort yet, especially not ones with enough authority to commandeer a direct delivery without being questioned.

"This doesn't point to Belle," he stated unequivocally, tossing the folder down. The pages fanned over his desk but he and Reece both ignored them.

"Her old man is in trouble—financially sinking and the cause is pretty much your fault," Reece said, his voice quiet with resignation. Mitch knew his cousin figured he'd just delivered the death knell to Mitch's relationship and felt rotten about it. "That deal the two of you cooked up, then you bailed on when your princess ran off has him tied up financially, and with real estate tanking, he's screwed with no way out."

"That sucks." And it did. Hugely. Mitch hadn't heard a whisper about it, but he wasn't surprised. Franklin Forsham was good at keeping things hush-hush. Regret washed over Mitch in a heavy wave. He'd been an asshole to leave Franklin in a lurch like that. Sure, he'd been humiliated and feeling justified in slapping out at anyone named Forsham, but the bottom line was it'd been bad business. He considered the current real estate climate, the tightened zoning laws in California and the probable debt Franklin had incurred holding the property all this time and winced.

"That totally sucks," he repeated. "But how does that make Belle the culprit in Lakeside's sabotage? In the first place, the problems started before she got here. Second and more significantly, she's under contract with me. The success of her business hinges on the success of my resort."

"Maybe. Or maybe she's more interested in her daddy's business right now." Reece grimaced, then pulled some more papers from that damned file. "I was chatting with Kiki, the gal who runs the spa here." In other words, flirting and looking for a good time. "Turns out Belle made her a very interesting proposition."

Mitch's mouth watered as he remembered the Brazilian treat he'd enjoyed the night before. "So?" he asked.

"It seems she's trying to lure Kiki away from your resort." Mitch's smile dropped away as Reece continued. "She's offering her gigs at her daddy's hotels. Same deal you have, but a few extra perks."

"That doesn't put her behind my resort issues."

"True," Reece agreed. Then he handed Mitch the papers he'd been holding. "Copies of the e-mails sent through the resort server from Belle to her partner."

Mitch started to point out how wrong it was to invade her e-mails when the words caught his eye.

The plan is in motion. Daddy will be thrilled.
Check timing of all of this. Can't let the cat out of the closet or Mitch will know.

Cat out of the closet. It was totally Belle-esque. His stomach fisted at the idea of her screwing him over with such calculation.

She'd walked out on him once without giving him the benefit of the doubt, not caring that she left him looking like an idiot. She was clever enough and resourceful enough to pull off revenge at this level and confident enough not to bat one long, mink eyelash.

But despite all the proof Reece was pitching, regardless of how many papers he stuffed in that file pointing the finger at Belle, Mitch wasn't going for it.

With a smile at odds with the subject, he settled back in his chair and finally identified the feeling he'd been struggling with since he'd walked into this office and seen his past waiting for him. He was in love with Belle. He had been six years ago, although he'd called it ambition. He was now, although he'd been trying to tell himself it was lust.

Love. Mitch shifted his gaze out the window to stare at the expanse of trees and gopher-infested lawn. Who knew it would feel so confusing?

But confusing or not, he loved her. Which meant, bottom line, he trusted her.

She might only be in this for the sex. She might still run away at any time, Mitch realized as his heart sank a little. He swallowed the bitter taste of fear at the possibility and told himself he'd deal with it later. The truth was, he wasn't blind to Belle's issues. But he knew screwing him at the same time she was screwing him over wasn't one of them.

"You're meeting with Belle tomorrow to talk security for the grand opening," he told Reece. "If you need to ask questions to make you feel like you're doing your job, go ahead. She's clean. But keep digging because the real culprit needs to be stopped before they do any more damage to my resort."

"You're gone, cuz." Reece shook his head in a pitying, you're-so-stupid kind of way.

"Totally gone," Mitch acknowledged, shoving aside the doubts. "And I'm loving every minute of it."

"I'VE GOT IT, the answer to our problem," Belle claimed in her daily phone call to Sierra. She tucked the cell between her chin and shoulder as she sliced a peach. They were now officially her favorite fruit.

"A blow-up doll with remote-control hands?" Sierra shot back.

Belle rolled her eyes at the phone. "Hardly. If we're using remote control I plan on operating something much more interesting than hands."

"Right. So what's our problem and then what's the answer?"

Sierra was usually so on top of things, but she'd been distracted during their last few phone calls, forgetting to send papers and contracts, just sort of disconnected from everything as far as Belle could tell.

Taking her snack to the table, Belle frowned in frustration. Questions were pointless. Sierra answered them all with annoying assurances that everything was just fine.

"Kiki's in," Belle explained. "She's really excited to take her spa to the next level and sees aligning with Forsham Hotels as the way to do it. Besides all the info I already sent you, I just found out she's courting a contract with one of the big-name beauty suppliers for an exclusive label."

"Do you think that's enough to help your dad?"

"I hope so. She'll pay top dollar for the square footage, but she'll also bring in a huge clientele. Between the label and her own promotion, they're going to skyrocket." Belle considered. "I have to convince Daddy, but if it works, he'll be able to switch all his on-site boutiques and stores. Rather than entities he runs and assumes the business expenses for, he can let his tenant take on the employee, inventory and liability risks. He'll cut his own expenses by at least an eighth."

Belle nibbled on her peach as they went on to brainstorm a few more ideas and kick around ways to pitch the proposal to her father. Finally deciding Belle would do it over Sunday brunch the next weekend, they wound up the topic.

"What about Lakeside?" Sierra asked. "Have you talked to Mitch about borrowing Kiki?"

"No," she said slowly. "I just didn't think it was a good idea until we'd worked out all the particulars."

"In other words, you don't want to rock the nookie boat until you're sure your dad's on board."

Belle was glad her shamed flush couldn't be seen over the phone.

"Kiki doesn't have an exclusivity contract," she defended.

"Doesn't mean Mitch expects her to be stolen away by his bed buddy."

"She's not being stolen. After she set things up here, she planned on leaving a manager in charge anyway. Besides," Belle justified, "it's good insurance for her. If someone really is playing some game here and the resort is going to suffer, she needs a safety net."

"Speaking of which, what'd you find out?" Sierra asked.

Glad to change the subject, Belle thought of the list she'd copied from Diana's office the day before. Someone was deliberately trying to ruin the resort. Was it Mitch? Despite the note and e-mail address, she couldn't believe it.

"It's not Mitch," she declared. "Why would he ruin his own venture? There just isn't anything in it for him. His board of directors is made up entirely of family. It's a family-held corporation, even."

"So?"

"So, nothing means more to him than family. This guy has a total *Brady Bunch* mindset."

"Are you sure you're not just trying to rationalize the fact that you're not done playing in his pants?" Sierra asked.

Pulling a face, Belle dropped to the couch and huffed out a

breath. "Do you really think sex is that important that I'd risk everything for it?"

"You did before."

Belle frowned. It wasn't sex, she wanted to say. It was Mitch. Just Mitch. Sex with him was her only excuse to intimacy, she realized. And didn't that make her a pitiful lovestruck idiot?

"Look, I need your input then. How'd you like to see the resort firsthand?" she asked after tucking her notes into her portfolio. "Come out, get a feel for the place, see Mitch in person and give me your opinion on what's what."

"You want me to come out there? Why? What'd you do?"

Belle rolled her eyes and made a huffing sound of irritation. "I didn't do anything. At least, nothing I need you to come fix. You have doubts about Mitch, I want your feedback. And I thought you'd enjoy getting the lay of the land, so to speak, before we kick into high gear next week preparing for the first event."

"Well, I'm grateful you don't want me to come fix your sex life," Sierra said with a laugh. "And you've already got a solid lay, so to speak, so I doubt you need me there."

"An upside-down head needs twice the help," Belle pointed out.

"Two heads are better than one," Sierra corrected with a sigh.

That she was desperate for Sierra to pinch hit for her in the security meeting wasn't going to fly as a reason, even if it was pure truth. She was totally freaked to face Reece alone. Even worse, she was terrified he'd ruin what she'd found with Mitch.

But she wasn't telling Sierra that.

"I'd love to have your take on who's tanking the resort, and maybe while you're here you can see if there's anything I could add for the first party, the one for Mitch's family and board, next week," Belle claimed instead. "I'm just a little nervous about pulling this off given that someone is trying to screw things up. It'd help to have a second set of eyes."

It was a flimsy ploy and she knew it. Belle orchestrated events for thousands on her own and never needed hand-holding. She cringed, waiting for her partner to call her on it and trying to figure out how to get out of dealing with Reece. Pretend to be sick? Really get sick? Family emergency and run home? She had to do something, anything. She so did not want to deal with the hot cowboy. Not when she knew he was just waiting to get her alone and confront her about the past.

"Okay, I can be there tomorrow morning," Sierra agreed after a long silence.

Belle kept her squeal of triumph to herself. "You can?"

"Sure. You want my help, I'll come give it. Why the shock? We're partners. That's what we do, help each other and tell each other crap."

Interesting theory, since Belle knew damned well Sierra was keeping *crap* from her. But confronting her friend was pointless, so Belle kept that a silent observation.

"Great." Never one to ruin a miracle by asking too many questions, Belle rushed on, "Since you'll be here anyway, you can take the meeting with the head of security and go over all the details, okay?"

"I should have known there was a catch." Sierra laughed. "Fine, I'll take the meeting."

Noting a movement out of the corner of her eye, Belle glanced out the window at the golf course. Mitch and Reece strode across the green expanse. Although both wore jeans and work shirts, the two men couldn't look more different. Yet they seemed to be solid friends in addition to having that family con-nection that was so important to Mitch.

Family. Since it was just her and her dad, Belle didn't quite get the whole clan feeling Mitch seemed to embrace. But she definitely knew how important it was to take care of her loved ones. Worrying over her father was proof of that.

Belle gave herself a second to appreciate Mitch's gorgeous ass, encased lovingly in denim, before she glanced at his leggy cowboy cousin. A sneaky plan formed in her head.

Six years ago she'd thought Sierra and Reece looked great together. Both tall, dark and gorgeous, they'd been striking at the pre-wedding festivities. If Reece had Sierra to distract him, it would keep him off Belle's back while she tried to figure out who was behind the dirty deeds at Mitch's resort.

It had nothing to do with the fact that Belle was so far gone over Mitch that she wanted everyone to experience the wonders of coupledom. Or if it did, she forced herself to admit, it was only because good sex was something her best friend deserved.

"Great," she told Sierra. "You're so much better at those details than I am and this security guy is hot. You'll have fun."

She figured Sierra was due for a hot, wild fling and Reece Carter was the perfect man to show her friend a sexy time. Belle couldn't wait to watch the sparks fly.

SPARKS, hell. It was like watching an inferno. Belle gaped as Sierra and Reece did everything but get naked and duke it out on the boardroom table.

"The resort has enough staff to handle the opening," Reece said in his long, slow drawl. "We don't need to bring in outside help and deal with more of those damned confidentiality agreements and clearances. Besides, how many people does it really take to serve a plate of mini hot dogs and tacos?"

"Don't worry about those mini hot dogs, cowboy," Sierra said with a wicked smile. "Nobody's going to hold yours against you. Besides, we figure the guests will have a little more refined taste. That means gourmet food, circulated while it's hot and fresh. And then there's the resort's theme—"

"Waste of time and money," he muttered, scrawling something over his notes. "People don't need silly games to have a good time."

Belle started to defend the themes and Mitch shifted his chair, leaning forward at the same time to comment. But before either could utter a word, Sierra gave a deep, patently fake sigh and shook her head.

With a pitying look, she tossed her long, dark hair over her shoulder and made a tut-tutting noise. "Are you afraid of games in sex, cowboy? Or is it the idea of other people coloring outside the lines that bothers you?"

"I'm all for a good time," he said with a look that made it clear to everyone in the room just how good a time he'd like to show Sierra. "It's when the good time veers out of easy and into complicated that I see it as a problem. Nobody should have to work for fun. Games just mess it all up."

Belle had the feeling she was missing half the conversation. The best half, if Sierra's breathless little laugh was anything to go by.

"As long as nobody's trying to slap handcuffs or nipple clips on you, what do you care?" Sierra asked. Then she gave him a taunting look. "Or are you afraid to play?"

"Sweetheart, I wrote the book on how to play. And," he said slowly, leaning across the table with a wicked grin, "how to win. You want a peek at a few pages, you just let me know."

"I'm trying to cut back on my fiction," Sierra told him with a wink.

Belle glanced at Mitch. He was staring, jaw slack, at the battle of verbal foreplay.

"So," Belle said bravely, breaking in to what should have been a simple security discussion. "I can see the two of you have this in hand so I'm going to take Mitch and do a walk-through of the weekend plans."

They ignored her.

Belle offered Mitch a helpless shrug. With one last look at the warring pair, now standing and facing off on either side of the table, she grabbed Mitch's hand and pulled him from the conference room.

As the door thudded shut behind them, Mitch started to ask a question. Before he could do more than mutter "oh, my God," they noticed Diana standing at the fax machine, her eyes huge.

"Guess you heard that," Belle said with a wince.

"Is everything okay?" the assistant asked quietly. "I needed your signature on some orders, Mitch, but it was so loud in there I figured I should wait."

"Security is a touchy issue," Mitch quipped as he strode over to take the file and pen from her.

Belle laughed and sat on the edge of Diana's desk to wait. She tried to think of something to say that would calm the other woman, who was visibly agitated, but all she could come up with were dirty jokes. Trying to get control of herself, she glanced away. Her gaze dropped to the computer monitor, where bubbles bounced across the screen.

Across the bottom of the open Word files was one with a stylized header. Belle noted how pretty the gold MC lettering was as the purple bubble shifted to turquoise. MC? Mitch's logo wasn't that girly, was it?

Before she could ask, he handed Diana back the papers and pen. "Stay out of the boardroom," he instructed his assistant as Belle joined him at the door. "If you hear furniture breaking, call the cops."

"But only furniture," Belle cautioned. "Groans, yells or screams should be ignored."

They were halfway down the hall before Mitch glanced at her in question. "Groans?"

"Oh please, they're so going to be doing it up against the wall before the day is over."

She'd taken another two steps before she realized he'd stopped cold.

"Doing it?" he asked blankly.

"*It*. The vertical vibration. The dirty deed. Riding the wild stallion. Bumping uglies." He still stared. Belle laughed and grabbed his hand to get him moving again. "Jeez, Mitch. What'd you think that was in there?"

"I thought it was hate at first sight," he muttered.

"With all that sexual innuendo? Hardly." They stopped at the front desk and Belle offered her thanks and a smile to Larry, who handed her a large picnic basket. Mitch took it from her and gestured for her to precede him out the door.

She waited until they were in the golf cart on their way to the woods to continue sharing her theory. "Heck, the sexual sparks and tension were so heavy back there I was getting turned on just being in the room."

"Are you sure that was them and not me?" he asked, glancing over as he steered the machine toward the trees. "I'd like to think you get hot and horny just being in the same room."

"You'd like to think that, hmm?" Belle laughed and patted his thigh before getting out of the now-stopped cart. "I admit, you do have a way of turning my thoughts to sexual escapades, whether you're in the room or not."

She reached for the basket, but he beat her to it. With a wink and a quick kiss, he gestured for her to step back and let him set up their lunch like the gentleman he was.

Belle settled against a tree trunk and looked out over the clearing, her entire being filled with a sense of peace and happiness she'd never felt before. She didn't know if it was the result of a week of incredible sex, her feelings for Mitch or the utter beauty of the woods. Whatever it was, she felt great.

She was curious though.

"Is your family going to have a problem with the sex angle?" she asked, watching him spread the thick red blanket over the lawn, then place the picnic basket on the corner before kicking off his shoes.

He laughed and held out his arm. Belle slipped off her sandals and settled on the blanket, where Mitch immediately grabbed her and rolled so she lay flat on top of him. He bunched the blanket up as a pillow and settled his hands on her waist with a sigh of contented pleasure.

"Believe me, my family has no issues with sex. From my youngest cousin to my gram, they're all pretty open-minded. Remember that list of sex-theme ideas I gave you? Those were straight from my family. Including this picnic, which was decidedly the tamest."

"Yeah," she said, her attention more focused on tracing his lips with her fingernail and reveling at the sweetness of the moment than their discussion. "There were some good ideas there. I tend to think a little bigger, and Sierra a little kinkier, so those were a nice balance."

"Kinkier? We left kinkier with my cousin?"

Delighted, Belle met his gaze and grinned. She was so in love, she realized. And even though it could be the biggest mistake of her life, right at this moment, she didn't care. She wanted to jump up, scream from the treetops how incredible Mitch was. Equal parts happiness and terror made her lightheaded. Okay, she realized as the ringing in her ears turned to a buzz, maybe the terror had an edge over the happiness.

There were so many reasons why this was insane. Why falling for Mitch was a horribly bad idea. Their history alone made believing they had a shot at happy-ever-after a total fairy tale.

But for right now, just this moment in time, she didn't care. She was giving happiness free rein and wringing every drop of joy from this interlude. And since joy translated so easily to sexual energy between them, she wiggled her hips a little. Mitch's body reacted instantly.

She melted at the humor in his cinnamon-sweet eyes and leaned closer. "That's okay. I've got bigger here with me," she said, referring back to his concern over his cousin being left with a kinky Sierra.

The humor left and Mitch's gaze went dark with desire. One hand slipped from Belle's waist down to cup her butt and press her tighter to him. The other combed through her hair.

"Why don't we see how much bigger we can get?" he said as he pulled her mouth to his.

Just before their lips met, Belle whispered, "And when we're done, I have a whole basket of aphrodisiacs there to prep you for the next round."

11

BELLE TRIED to stop her hands from shaking as she carefully lowered herself into Diana's office chair.

"It's not booby-trapped, you know," Sierra hissed from the door where she was standing lookout. "Just sit down and get to it."

Belle rolled her eyes at her partner in crime. Her exasperation was more calming than the deep-breathing exercise she'd been trying since they'd decided to break into Mitch's assistant's office.

Her stomach constricted again.

No, *break in* was the wrong term. It was business hours. Broad daylight. Just because Belle had carefully timed her visit to coincide with Mitch's trip to the airport and had arranged for Diana to pick up a special order that suddenly couldn't be delivered didn't mean it was wrong.

"Get on with it," Sierra snapped. "We don't have that much time."

Belle glared, but before she could say anything, her lookout did a hurry-up motion with her hand. Figuring finger gestures were next, Belle bit the bullet and, with a cringe, started peeking into file folders.

"You're positive she's the dirty dog who's screwing Mitch over?" Sierra asked as Belle carefully repositioned the laundry invoices in their file.

"No," Belle shot back. "I already told you, I'm not positive. But every bit of evidence I've found has been right here in her office. And since I refuse to believe it's Mitch himself, that leaves her. Now stop bugging me and keep watch."

Finished with the folders on the desk and not brave enough to start on drawers, Belle moved the mouse beside Diana's computer. The floating bubble screen saver cleared and her gaze flew to the bottom of the screen. Of course, there was no incriminating document open today. Clueless but determined, she randomly opened and scanned document files. While she did, she considered the question. At least Sierra had stopped arguing that it might be Mitch. After meeting him again, spending the last few days in his company, she'd been totally won over.

The same couldn't be said for her opinion of Reece, Belle had noticed. After that first explosive meeting four days ago, they'd retreated behind a wall of polite iciness. So much for sexual tension. Instead of being engulfed in heat, they'd straight up frozen each other out. When she'd tried asking Sierra about it, her friend had claimed instant irritation as the culprit and stated she was taking the high road and ignoring the idiot.

Frustration built as the seconds ticked and Belle came up empty-handed. Sierra hissed. Terror slapped Belle and her gaze flew to the door. Instead of a bust, though, Sierra made another hurry-up gesture. Belle opened her mouth to retort but Sierra put her finger to her lip for silence and raised both brows. She was having way too much fun with this covert crap.

With a curl of her lip, Belle mentally flipped her friend off, then went back to her snooping. Her silent cuss-fest halted when she found the recycling bin and stabbed the mouse button to open it.

Gobbledygook. Most of the files had recognizable names, but a few were weird combinations of numbers and symbols. All had the current date. Did that mean Diana emptied the recycle bin daily? The extent of Belle's computer knowledge ended when she hit Send on her e-mail, so she had no clue. She clenched her teeth in a silent scream of frustration. She should have let Sierra check the computer, but if one of them was going to get caught, Belle needed to take responsibility.

Helpless to do anything else, she started opening random files.

And found what she was looking for in her third gobbledygook.

"Holy shit," she whispered as she read.

"What?"

Belle waved Sierra to silence as she right-clicked, trying to find the print command.

"Belle," Sierra muttered.

"I'll tell you in a second," she said, brows furrowed as she tried to find the print icon. She hated this new operating system, she had no idea where anything was.

Aha. She clicked.

"No." Sierra's words had gone from a hiss to full-out panic. "Now—you have to move now."

"What?" Panic was a stifling blanket of intense black heat as it poured over Belle. Her gaze flew to the printer, spewing pages, and back to Sierra's freaked-out face.

"That damned cowboy is coming up the hall," Sierra hissed, her eyes flitting around for someplace to hide.

"Damn."

Belle stood so fast the chair flew back and hit the wall. But the move didn't make the printer spew any faster. How long was that file? She gnawed at her lip, dancing in place. Did she hit Stop and leave it in the queue, tipping Diana off? Did she grab and run? Did she...

She caught herself actually wringing her hands and gave a little scream of frustration at the printer.

"Hold him off," she ordered.

"What? You're crazy."

She glared at Sierra and pointed toward the hallway. "Now. Get his attention, drag him off to look at a horse or something. I don't give a damn what you do, but keep him out of here."

Sierra huffed and glared. But Belle watched thankfully as she turned on her heel and with a quick shake of her shoulders sashayed down the hall. As the door swung shut behind her, Belle sent up a brief prayer for the cowboy's virtue and cleared the files from the computer screen. Finally, the last page printed. She grabbed the stack of papers, folded them and then looked down. A-line skirt, camp shirt, sassy heels. No purse, no pockets, no hiding place.

She glanced at her breasts. Too small, shirt too tight not to notice the sharp angle of folded pages. Oh to be a C-cup and have hiding room.

With another glance at the door and knowing that as good as Sierra was, if he wanted in this office, Reece would be storming in any moment, she slid the pages into the waistband of her skirt right at the small of her back. Tucking her shirt over the top of them, she winced and realized she'd have to walk sideways down the hall to keep them hidden. Of all the times to forget her portfolio.

But a girl had to do what a girl had to do. So she smoothed a shaking hand over her hair, pasted her biggest fake smile on and headed for the door. Opening it just a smidge, she peeked out.

Nothing. No Sierra, no Reece. Belle frowned and tried to angle herself to peek the other way. Still nothing.

Had Sierra really dragged him off to see a horse?

Did she care? Nope, Belle just heaved a sigh of relief, and with a quick grab for an empty file folder on the cabinet, retrieved the pages from her skirt, tucked them in and opened the door.

She couldn't wait to get back to her cottage to see who was behind the dirty deeds. Belle grinned, gave a finger wave at the concierge and practically skipped through the foyer. Wouldn't Mitch love her when he realized she'd saved him, too? Hey, she'd take any way she could to get into his heart.

MITCH WATCHED the rush of bodies hurrying through Lakeside's foyer in satisfaction. Waitstaff bringing food to the registration desk for the guests. At the concierge station, uniformed men were polishing the brass of the luggage carts. Housekeeping was running a damp mop over the marble and berating the waiter for dropping a crumb. Mitch grinned. Crazy busy preparation for the party that night. He loved it.

"What do you think?" he asked Larry, who was checking items off some list in a frantic way. The only person Mitch knew who was more list-obsessed was Belle. Totally beyond his comprehension, but he was damned grateful for the results.

"Timing, check. Food, check. Housekeeping, check. Flowers… where are the flowers?" Larry asked in a panicked tone.

Mitch nudged him, then pointed to the bouquets flanking the registration desk and the three people setting other arrangements around the foyer. His manager's lips moved as he counted them. Then he nodded and made a mark on his clipboard.

Assured that things were under control, Mitch grinned and slapped Larry on the shoulder before heading over to the desk to sample the appetizers.

Before he could eat more than one brie-stuffed mushroom, Reece strode up, his face set in hard lines. He reminded Mitch of a gunfighter taking his stance to draw.

"What's wrong?" Mitch asked when his cousin came closer. "Did you have a row with one of the cousins already?"

The investors, aka their entire family, had been arriving all day for tonight's event. He'd been fielding congratulations and backslaps all afternoon and he was loving it.

"We need to talk."

Mitch's smile didn't falter. He was in too good a mood to be worried about his cousin's recent doom-and-gloom attitude.

"So talk."

"Privately."

"Look, I don't have time for a covert exchange of information. I've got a lot going on here, in case you didn't notice. The entire family flew in. I picked Grammy Lynn up at the airport a couple hours ago. She's up in her room now laughing over the sex toys. The party is in three hours, so you should think about getting yourself ready."

In other words, Mitch didn't want to deal with this shit now. His focus was the party, a small-scale practice run for the special invitation to the press and A-listers grand opening starting the next week. They were still serving an aphrodisiac-inspired menu, hiring a live band for dancing and inviting couples to participate in the sex-themed offerings. But as much as he loved them, Mitch didn't think his family would appreciate caviar and Cristal. Not when they knew the costs came out of their investment.

"Belle was in your office," Reece said in a low voice.

"So?"

"Snooping around, using the computer." Reece's tone changed. "Her and that high-maintenance friend of hers."

Mitch sighed. "Again with Sierra? You don't have to maintain her, so what's the problem."

"No woman is worth the energy it'd take to maintain that one," Reece mused. He rocked back on his heels and shoved his hands in the front pockets of his jeans while he contemplated the idea. "Although she's one helluva short, sweet ride."

"Giddyap," Mitch muttered as he took the clipboard from Larry. After glancing at the liquor-delivery invoice, he signed his name and returned it with a nod of thanks. "You said *is?*"

Pulled out of his reverie, Reece stared blankly. "Huh?"

"*Is* a wild ride. Not *would be,* not *seems like. Is.* Care to fill me in?"

His cousin stood stock-still, no expression on his usually affable face. Then he shrugged.

"That's not the point," Reece stated. "Those women had no reason to be in there. I think they were up to something."

Mitch sighed.

"Look," Reece said, stepping around so he was face-to-face with Mitch. "You don't want to believe it, that's fine. But security is my job. Let me do it my way."

"Do what your way? Giddyap?"

Reece's eyes flashed rare anger. Mitch braced himself, even though he knew the punch wasn't coming. His cousin never lost his temper.

"Mitch," called a woman's voice.

Both men glanced over to watch a stunning, heavyset woman cross the foyer in khaki capris and a white military-style shirt.

"Lena, you made it," Mitch greeted, glad to see his stepsister. They exchanged a hug before she turned to Reece and, a hand on either bicep, pulled him close for a half hug.

"Royce, how are you?" she asked. She tossed her dark hair behind her shoulder and gave him a toothy smile.

"It's Reece, and I'm doing pretty good. It's nice to see you again."

Mitch doubted that. Reece had complained more than once about Lena back when Mitch's stepdad and mom had been alive. The two families hadn't blended well, though not for lack of trying on the adults' part. But Lena hadn't ever quite fit with

Mitch's bevy of cousins. Reece in particular had developed a tendency to leave the room as soon as she entered. Probably because she'd thought he was—how'd she put it? Mitch frowned then remembered. The bomb.

He gave a silent laugh and watched her pour the charm on his cousin and realized that whatever was bugging Reece must be major, since he wasn't excusing himself to leave.

Apparently Reece's monosyllabic responses outweighed his appeal as the bomb, so, after a minute of attempting to catch up, Lena turned her attention back to Mitch.

"I'm so excited for you. I just took myself on a tour around the grounds and, wow, Mitch. This is one gorgeous property."

"Thanks."

They discussed the resort's amenities while Reece loomed like a silent nag behind them. Since she wasn't an actual investor or on the board, Mitch hadn't considered Lena when he'd told Diana to arrange for his entire family to come out. He rarely saw the other woman, but since he'd loved her father and the old man had always been there for him, he'd readily approved her addition to the guest list.

"It's so great to see you both," Lena gushed again. "But I'm going to go ahead and pretend I'm a posh guest here and do the registration thing, then relax a little bit before the fancy soiree this evening."

The men offered their goodbyes, and, as Lena turned to leave, she tossed an invitation over her shoulder. "Reece, you be sure and save me a dance. I'd love to revisit old times."

"Old times?" Mitch teased under his breath as she left.

"Whatever," he muttered back.

Mitch laughed in delight. This was going to be one helluva fun evening.

"You need to let me do my job," Reece said when they were alone again.

Mitch shrugged. "We've been through this already. Go ahead, do your job. But don't screw with my event and don't be making any unfounded accusations. You nail someone, you better be damned sure you have the right person and enough proof to make a case."

"You'll have your proof by the end of the night," Reece assured him.

The words were right, but the feeling in Mitch's stomach was all kinds of wrong.

BELLE DISCONNECTED her cell phone and was just tossing it in her evening bag when Sierra came into the cottage.

"What took you so long?" she asked. "We're due on-site in five minutes."

She spent ten seconds admiring her partner's vintage Vera Wang dress before she glanced at Sierra's face. Belle frowned.

"You're chewing on your lip," she mumbled.

"So?"

The brunette's tone was not only confrontational, it had do-not-disturb vibes all around it. Belle wanted to know what had happened that afternoon, where Sierra had hauled Reece off to, that kind of thing. But it didn't take a half-assed Sherlock Holmes like herself to put two and two together and realize wherever it was, whatever they'd done, Sierra wasn't happy about it.

"So, nothing," Belle said, backing down. No point in starting a fight. "Do you want to see what I found?"

Sierra took one eager step forward then grimaced and shook her head. "We don't have time. Give me the summary."

"The file was a detailed list of instructions on how to cause trouble for the resort. Everything from those animals in the golf course to the cancelled meat order are listed there."

"Diana typed up a list?" Sierra's tone made it clear how dumb she thought that was.

"No, they're instructions from the person she works for." Belle checked her hair in the mirror one last time and adjusted the strap of her ice-blue evening dress. Bias-cut silk, it hugged her curves in ways she hoped Mitch appreciated. "Apparently she's supposed to delete any files from the computer each day, too. Thanks for the idea to send her on that wild goose chase to pick up the replacement supplies. Otherwise she'd have emptied the recycle bin and I wouldn't have proof."

"Who's behind it?"

Belle paused, still trying to believe it herself. Then she shrugged and said with a frown, "L.N. Larry Nelson. Mitch's manager."

"No," Sierra breathed, her blue eyes wide with shock. "He seems so geeky and devoted. Are you sure?"

Belle cringed at the question. She felt so defensive even making the accusation. Like a traitorous bitch.

"I don't have proof positive," she defended. "But his name is mentioned here and these are his initials. He's also on the access list and was involved with the computer crash."

"That's pretty sketchy," Sierra pointed out with a grimace. "Remember at one point you thought it might be Mitch based on that first note?"

"I never believed it was Mitch," Belle defended angrily.

"Right, I know. But it looked like it. All I'm saying is this isn't enough to hold up in court, if you know what I mean."

"I know." Belle's defensiveness dropped away. She thought of the list. Only half the items on it had been crossed off. Some looked like they were supposed to take place after the grand opening. The ones about contacting the paparazzi would ruin the resort.

She shoved a hand through her curls and tried to think straight. They were silent for a few seconds, Belle trying to figure out how to tell Mitch what she'd found and wondering how angry he'd be with her for snooping, Sierra undoubtedly imagining how this was going to affect their contract.

"Have you told him yet?"

"Told Mitch?" Belle's stomach tensed again, fear dulling her anger. She swallowed twice before answering. "No, I haven't had a chance yet."

"But you're going to, right? As soon as you see him?" Sierra's face set in stubborn lines.

"I'll tell him later," Belle hedged. Her friend glared. "What? I'm supposed to grab him just before the party he's throwing for his entire family and tell him to turn around so I can point out the knives two of his most trusted employees shoved in his back? Warned is unarmed, as they say."

"Forewarned is forearmed," Sierra said with a roll of her eyes. "That's stupid. You're sidestepping the confrontation. Just talk to the man, Belle. You get naked and eat fruit off each other, for God's sake. You can tell him."

"I was talking to my dad just before you came in," Belle said, changing the subject. Sierra sighed, but didn't say anything. Belle ignored her blatant disapproval. She wasn't going to push for a confrontation at the party. That'd be crazy. She'd wait until tomorrow, sit down with Mitch and show him the proof. She took two deep breaths to calm her nausea and focused on distracting Sierra.

"He met with Kiki and they're good to go. He's offered her space in two of his hotels for her spa and he took your suggestion to make the same offer to some boutiques. He even has a meeting on Monday with Cartier and Tiffany's to bring in some bling."

Sierra paused in reapplying her lipstick to grin, genuine pleasure edging out the disapproval in her bright-blue eyes. "That rocks. It sounds like he figures this is the right track?"

"His people crunched some numbers and estimate the changes

will keep things afloat until the real estate market levels and he can get out from under that property."

"And..." Sierra shot her a long, narrow look. "You're nervous about something. Is he okay?"

Belle bit her own lip now and pressed her hand to her stomach to calm the flutters. "I invited him to the main event."

"Here?" Her eyes huge, Sierra gave a silent whistle. "Did you tell him whose resort you're opening? Aren't you afraid of an ugly public blowup?"

"I told him. He was..." *Ugly* would be the best word. But Belle had stood up to him. She'd almost puked, but she'd stood her ground. "I told him I'm serious about Mitch and they need to mend the fence I kicked down. He agreed to go to dinner with Mitch and me next week."

Sierra dropped her lipstick into her beaded black purse and the two women made their way out the door. "Mitch is cool with this?"

Belle wrinkled her nose. "I hope. I'll ask him over whipped cream."

The two women walked through the garden, lit with fairy lights, past the fountain with its cushioned benches and into the ballroom.

Staff was putting last-minute touches on the flowers and lighting candles at the small tables around the room. The bar staff was setting up the champagne fountain while two bartenders organized their stations on either side of the room.

"You need to tell him," Sierra said as they stood in the entrance.

"You need to back off," Belle shot back. "If we're going to play show and tell, maybe you could fill me in on the cowboy?"

Silence.

Then her friend shrugged and shook out the skirt of her dress.

"It looks good, everything is on schedule," Sierra said with a glance at her watch. "An hour till show time?"

"Yep," Belle agreed. "You're in charge of keeping an eye on Larry."

Sierra wrinkled her nose, but nodded. "Let's rock this party."

And later tonight, after a vigorous bout of hot, sweaty sex, Belle would tell Mitch his assistant was in cahoots with his manager to destroy his resort.

12

"LADIES AND gentlemen, welcome to Lakeside," Belle said from the raised dais, the microphone carrying her words to the glittering corners of the ballroom. "You're all going to enjoy an incredible stay at this gorgeous luxury resort, and for you couples here, you're in for one wild time."

Mitch watched the nudges spread around the room and grinned. Belle was like a sexy fairy up there on stage, wooing and entertaining his family and friends. She described the features of the resort and the quote-unquote "normal" special events they had planned for the next three days.

"And for those, shall we say, more adventurous among you," she added, her tone changing from charming to flirtatious, "we've got a few special treats."

Her emphasis on *special* had the room laughing. "As you know, Lakeside is going to be much more than a posh vacation spot for the rich and famous. Only at Lakeside can paparazzi-weary A-listers come for complete and total privacy. For relaxation. For romance. And best of all, for great sex."

At her last words, the entire room broke into applause. Belle waited for the wave of chatter to die down before going on to describe some of the more exotic extras the resort would offer. She also listed a choice few the guests would be able to sample for themselves tonight.

Mitch's grandma elbowed him in the side and lifted her champagne flute. "Good job, sweetie. She's got style."

"She came up with a great plan for the success of the resort," he said, unable to take his eyes off Belle as she descended from the stage and stopped to speak to Larry, then to Sierra, who for some bizarre reason had been clinging to the manager all evening. Mitch liked Larry well enough, but wondered if he should warn him about Belle's business partner. If Reece couldn't handle the giddyup kink of that sultry brunette, there was no way Larry could.

Belle, looking serious and intense, was speaking to some guy Mitch didn't recognize. Must be one of her people, he guessed. Mitch's gaze slid over her tousled blond curls and he sighed. Damn, even in a room filled with glitz and glitter, she still sparkled.

"She's caught your eye again, that's for sure," Grammy Lynn noted.

Mitch just shrugged. Why deny the obvious? He tore his gaze from Belle to look around for Reece. His cousin was at the far end of the room talking to one of the security guys. Mitch frowned. Had something else gone wrong? He caught Reece's eye and raised a brow in question. Reece gave an infinitesimal shake of his head and nodded toward the lake, visible outside the open French doors.

Good. Preparation for the tour details. The tension left Mitch's shoulders as he returned the nod. Just then, Belle sauntered over, a gorgeous smile lighting her face.

"Phase one complete," she said, sounding happy. A tiny purse dangled from her wrist and Mitch had to wonder if she had one of her infamous lists all folded up in there. She offered his grandmother a warm smile and said hello, reminding Mitch that he was being rude.

He reintroduced the two women, feeling a little ashamed about the last time they'd met—the non-event of their wedding.

"I was just complimenting my grandson on how well you've put this all together," his grandmother told Belle after the introductions. "When he first mentioned this to the board, I was worried it'd be tacky. You know, like that penis confetti at my niece Jenny's twenty-first birthday party."

He grinned at Belle's wince when Grammy Lynn said *penis*. For such a sexually adventurous woman, Belle was oddly prim in some situations. Satisfaction and happiness settled around him like a comfy blanket as Mitch watched his grandmother and Belle fall into an enthusiastic discussion. In five minutes, they covered parties, the perfect cake and, as Belle's initial inhibitions faded, the right way to display condoms.

Before they could start exchanging sex tips, he laid a hand on Belle's forearm and gave his grandmother a warm smile.

"We need to start the tour," he told his ladies. *His ladies.* He liked the sound of that. Knowing the message it'd give, he slid his hand down Belle's arm to wrap his fingers around hers. She shot him a panicked look and subtly tried to shake his hand off, but he didn't let go.

"So it's like that, is it?" his grandmother said in satisfaction.

"No."

"Yes."

They answered at the same time, then Belle gave him one of those what-are-you-doing-are-you-crazy? looks. Before he could say anything else, she unwrapped his fingers from hers so she could put her hand out to shake Grammy's.

"I'm not… We're just…" She glared at Mitch. He just rocked back on his heels and grinned. "It was a pleasure talking with you, Lynn. I'd love to have brunch tomorrow and hear more of your ideas."

With that and one last searing glance at Mitch, she gathered the silky fabric of her skirt in her hand and swept away.

"You gonna make it to the vows this time?" Grammy asked.

Belle subtly crooked her finger at a waiter, who immediately approached her, carrying a large crystal dish on a tray. Mitch watched her hand each set of guests who'd signed up for the sex-theme tour an envelope. She spent a few minutes with each couple, chatting, putting them at ease with her jokes and natural warmth. Damn, she worked the room as easily as she'd worked his heart.

"You bet," he said, his gaze still locked on the sweet sway of Belle's hips as she moved between couples. "I'm a lot smarter this time."

HER SMILE large enough that she figured her cheeks would ache in the morning, Belle handed the second-to-last envelope to one of Mitch's cousins and his very pregnant wife.

"I've been looking forward to this weekend for months," the petite redhead told her as her husband tore into the envelope. "But when Jase told me about this little sideline, I'll admit, I went into impatience overload."

She leaned closer and dropped her voice to a whisper. "This last trimester has me so horny, Jase is going to have to go on early paternity leave to keep up with me."

"I had no idea pregnancy had such a stimulating side effect," Belle said, intrigued. Before she could decide if she wanted more details or not, Jase showed his wife the invitation. From the looks of it, they'd drawn the rose garden adventure. Pure fairy-tale fantasy, complete with a rose bower and fairy lights. Belle gave a silent sigh of relief. As horny as she seemed, Belle doubted a ride in a golf cart over a gopher-ravaged golf course at night was good foreplay for a pregnant lady.

With a giggle and a promise to chat the next day, the couple hurried out of the ballroom. Belle smiled and gave a rueful shake of her head. She felt like a madam sending her couples off for a night of decadent debauchery.

This whole evening was incredible. She loved Mitch's family. Fun, easygoing and interesting, they'd all welcomed her as if the wedding fiasco six years ago had never happened. Well, all except that one weird guy who'd tried to get her to agree to meet him for a private talk when she'd left the dais.

One last envelope to go. She had no idea what the sexual treat hidden in the heavy card stock was, but she couldn't wait to find out. She saw Sierra across the room holding court among the single guys, including Larry, and headed that way.

She'd made it halfway when she came face-to-face with her worst nightmare. Belle's vision wavered as fury hit. The woman who'd ruined her wedding. Belle wanted to scratch her eyes out.

Pleasant and distant, she told herself. This wasn't the time or place to tell Mitch's stepsister what a nasty, rotten bitch she was. Belle clenched her teeth so tightly she thought they'd crack and forced a smile on her face.

"Well, well," drawled the stocky brunette. "I'd heard you were in charge of this little sexcapade, but I thought it was the family's idea of a joke. What kind of kinky things did you have to do to con Mitch into trusting you?"

"Lena," Belle said, her voice pure ice in an attempt to smother the fiery anger. "I'm surprised to see you here. You have an odd habit of showing up at Mitch's celebrations with an eye toward ruining them."

The other woman gave her a toothy grin and looked around the room with a disdainful shrug that shifted her blue beaded evening dress in unattractive ways.

"This party is already doomed. Why would I waste energy?"

"Doomed, is it?" Unable to help herself, Belle stepped forward until she was close enough to smell Lena's oversweet perfume. "Why would you say that?"

Lena's brown eyes narrowed and she flipped her hair over her shoulder with a look of disgust. "It's a no-brainer, isn't it?

You're in charge." She arched her brow. "Things are bound to be unfinished. Did you plan to escape before or after the champagne runs dry?"

Belle hissed.

"Ladies, dessert is being served," Sierra said, her tone dulcet. The hand on Belle's waist squeezed in warning. "Lena, why don't you go on in? I'm afraid I need Belle's help for just a second."

After a ten-second stare-down, the woman shrugged and left. It was all Belle could do to keep herself from going after her.

"Well, this is a fine turnaround," Sierra said with a tense laugh as Lena flounced away. "You looking like you were going to kick her ass and me being the voice of reason."

"Scary," Belle agreed as she tried to shake off her anger.

"You can't go after her," Sierra cautioned. "You're too emotional. If you blow up, it'll make you look like a fool and ruin the event." Sierra's voice trailed off and she gave a quick glance around. Nobody was paying any attention to them, so she just shrugged and said, "You have a fit and you'll play right into her hands. You've won over Mitch's family, and that's saying a lot considering they all thought you should have been strung up for leaving him. Don't ruin that. Just avoid her."

Mitch.

Belle took a deep breath and smoothed a hand over her silk-covered hip. With a second deep breath she looked around to find him in conversation with Reece. She pressed her lips together to try to keep from growling and forced the anger aside.

"Escape, my ass," she muttered, clenching the envelope in her fist. She gave Sierra an angry shrug and instructed, "Cover the dessert reception, please."

Then she stormed across the room to get her man.

"Belle, no," Sierra warned, hurrying to keep up with her. "Do not ruin this event. You'll regret it."

Belle kept going.

"Don't let her win. Again."

Belle stopped so fast she was surprised there wasn't smoke coming off her Manolos. "She ruined my wedding."

"No." Sierra stepped around Belle so they were face-to-face and gave her a long, serious look. Her voice was low and apologetic. "She didn't. She pushed the buttons, but the problems were already there. You know that."

Belle was about to protest, but when her friend just raised a brow, she dropped her gaze to the marble floor. Sierra was right. Belle didn't want her to be, but she was. Belle had ruined her own wedding, pure and simple. Shame washed over her as she blinked to clear the tears from her eyes. She wanted to leave, to go to her cottage, curl up under a blanket with Mr. Winkles and pout. But she couldn't. This wasn't the time or place to have a girly breakdown. Mitch was counting on her, and she was counting on herself.

"Okay, you're right. She didn't do anything," Belle finally conceded.

Sierra's arched brows drew together over angry blue eyes. "Oh no, I didn't say that. She's a selfish, conniving bitch and we're going to haul her out to the woods and kick her ass when this is all over."

Belle's surprised laugh faded as she watched Lena and Diana greet each other like long-lost friends. A quick hug and the two women put their heads together, talking at the same time. She'd had no idea they even knew each other. Were she and Sierra the only ones in the room not family or close friends?

Before Belle could speculate, a hand curved over her hip and someone dropped a kiss on the side of her neck. With a gasp of surprise, she spun around. It was Mitch, of course. Who else would it be? she asked herself as she tried to calm her racing heart.

"What?" he said with a laugh. "You two look all guilty. Like you're planning to rob a bank. Or…" He glanced around the room, then noted the envelope in Belle's hand. He reached out so they held it together. "…talking sex."

"Definitely sex," Sierra agreed with a nod. She puffed out a little breath, her only sign of nerves, and gave Mitch a warm smile. "And speaking of sex, if you'll excuse me, there's a man I'm interested in."

Belle wanted to grab Sierra back and force her to stay with them until she'd got her thoughts under control. Between worrying that Diana and company had some trap planned for the evening and the shock of seeing Lena the bitch again, Belle's nerves were shot.

"Care to share?" Mitch said in a low, sexy tone as he leaned closer.

"Um, share what?"

He laughed again and moved her hand. She glanced at the envelope and grimaced. As hot as Mitch was in a tux, for the first time since she'd set eyes on him, she wasn't interested in having sex with him.

"You know, it's probably tacky for the host and the event planner to sneak off and have nookie," she said, giving him a wide-eyed look.

"It's a nookie kind of night," he pointed out. He slid an appreciative look up and down the length of her body. Belle felt as if he'd stripped her naked and licked his way down to her toes. Hot, damp excitement sparked inside her. "And there are no peaches on the dessert menu."

Unable to say no when he gave her that cute, little-boy grin, Belle giggled and released her hold on the envelope. "You're going to have to give other fruits a chance, you know."

"Nah, why mess with perfection? Besides, I have a bowl of peaches waiting in my room for later," he promised, his attention on ripping open the envelope. When he read the card inside, a huge grin split his face. "The lake? In a boat? Right on."

So in love it hurt, Belle burst into laughter, and even though she knew she should suggest they go to his office and talk, she let him whisk her out of the room.

MITCH FELT damned good. He'd impressed the hell out of his family with the resort. The party had rocked. And now he was taking his woman out to play water games. Life didn't get much better than this.

"Wow," he said as they approached the lake. The long, wooden dock was lined on either side with jars, each one containing a flickering candle. Rather than a motorboat, she'd gone the safer route and had a large rowboat tied to the end of the dock. As they got closer, Mitch could see there was a bottle of champagne chilling, glasses and what looked like some kind of dessert.

"Peaches?" he asked hopefully.

Belle grinned and shook her head. "Chocolate-covered strawberries."

Mitch watched her balance on one foot, her hand on his arm as she slipped off one shoe, then the other, before stepping onto the grass. He took the strappy sandals from her and, dangling them from one finger, clasped her hand in his and led the way to paradise.

He wasn't sure if she was tired after all her work on the party or if someone had upset her, but Belle seemed a little distant and disconnected, as though she didn't mind humoring him, but would rather be anywhere else but here.

Wanting to help her relax, he dropped her shoes in the grass and wrapped his arms around her. One kiss turned into two, deepening as Mitch lost himself in the glory of her mouth. He felt the tension leave her body as Belle relaxed and leaned into him, her tongue dancing around his in sensual delight.

Mitch's hands curved over the smooth fabric of her dress, smoothing his way down her hips and over her butt. She drove him crazy. He pulled her close to grind his hardening dick against her silky warmth.

Releasing her mouth, he trailed wet kisses over her jaw, down her throat. When he reached the curve of her neck, Mitch buried his face there and breathed in the delicious scent of her.

He slipped the tiny straps of her dress off her shoulders, his mouth giving the delicious peak of her breast a nibble. Before he could do the same to the other breast, he was blinded by a flashing light.

"Do her on the grass," a male voice yelled. Insults and degrading suggestions flew through the air.

More lights. Click and whir. Belle screamed. Mitch pulled away, pushing her behind him as he tried to see into the dark woods. Fists clenched, he ran forward to find out what was going on. Before he could take more than three steps, a golf cart flew across the lawn, grass flying behind it as it suddenly braked.

Wrapping a protective arm around a shaking Belle, Mitch watched his cousin Reece leap from the cart and grab someone at the edge of the woods.

"Oh my God," Belle breathed as they watched him do some intense martial arts move and kick an object from the guy's hand. Then with a flying leap, he sent the other person flying backward, where he smacked into a tree with a loud thud.

Two more golf carts flew by, security staff jumping out to grab the guy and haul him over to Mitch. Reece sauntered over, scooping up his dropped cowboy hat on the way and smacking the dirt off it before putting it back on his head.

Mitch almost laughed at his cousin's nonchalant attitude, then he caught sight of the creep being held by the scruff of his jacket.

"Who the hell are you?" Mitch demanded. He wanted to haul off and punch the guy in the face, but the idiot was still dazed and bleeding from his lip, thanks to Reece's roundhouse kick.

Dammit, his cousin got to have all the fun. Mitch consoled himself with the promise that he'd have one hell of a time prosecuting the guy.

"Don't worry about that," Reece said. "The question isn't so much who he is but who called him out here."

"Paparazzi?" Belle asked in a small voice, sounding shaken by the lightning-fast change from passion to violence. God, Mitch thought, if the guy had shown up ten minutes later, his shots would have been X-rated.

Obviously thinking the same thing, Belle took a deep breath and seemed to be fighting the need to cry. She gave Mitch a watery smile. "At least he didn't get any incriminating shots, right?"

Mitch frowned, but before he could reply, his cousin stepped between them.

"What if it had been someone else? This is exactly what you're promising your guests they'll be protected from, isn't it?" Reece stepped close and dangled the broken camera pieces from his index finger. "This could have been any one of our family members. While I'm sure cousin Jenny's lakeside frolics wouldn't make headlines like some movie star's, it'd be pure misery for her to see them splashed across a gossip rag."

"This is what security was supposed to prevent," Belle snapped. "All those meetings, all our discussions. Confidentiality agreements, key codes, alarms. And yet this dirtbag still managed to get in here? This entire plan hinged on the guarantee of privacy. What the hell happened?"

"Someone tipped him off," Mitch accused. Fury blurred his vision at the betrayal. He stepped forward and grabbed the guy's collar.

"Who the hell hired you?" he growled.

The guy muttered through swollen lips, "The party gal."

Shocked, Mitch almost dropped him. "Belle?"

"Don't know her name. Just had the phone call that this was some big fancy A-lister gig with a lot of money shots. Sex, partying. I was told to come on out. She put my name on the guest list, texted me to tell me where to hide."

No. Mitch reeled at the words. Reece grabbed the guy from his slack hands and wheeled him around.

"Bullshit," Reece claimed. "You're saying Belle Forsham hired you? Tipped you off? What?"

"Don't know her name. Just that she's the gal in charge of the party" the guy snapped defiantly. "We talked by phone, e-mail. I never saw her before."

"He's lying," Belle called out. Horror filled her voice, tears glistening on her cheeks.

"Why would he lie?" Reece wondered aloud.

"I don't know," Belle cried. "Why don't you ask him?"

"I don't think we need to ask anyone except you, Ms. Forsham." Reece's words were quiet, bland. But his accusation hung in the air.

"Me? Why the hell would I do this?" Anger snapped in her eyes.

"You could be working to discredit the resort," Reece said in his slow drawl. "Your dad's hurting, needs money. You might have thought putting Mitch out of business would keep away some competition."

Belle shook her head. "You might want to go back to security school, cowboy. So far you're batting zip. First you let that camera-toting idiot in here, despite all the supposed precautions. Then you accuse me of something impossibly far-fetched. This resort is no competition to my father."

"Sure it isn't," muttered someone behind Mitch. "She

screwed him over once, she's obviously doing it again. This time she's getting pictures, too."

Belle gasped, her eyes filling. But instead of letting the tears fall, she lifted her chin and faced the crowd that had formed around them.

Shaking off the feeling of fury and betrayal, Mitch followed her gaze and saw her glare at Lena. Mitch frowned. He glanced at his stepsister, whose grin looked evil in the glinting moonlight. Belle opened her mouth as if to say something, then she shrugged and turned to leave.

"Where do you think you're going?" he asked.

"Away." He could hear it in her voice, the need to escape. To get away from the whispers and judgmental eyes.

"This isn't settled, Belle."

She gave him a dirty look. "What's to settle? Did you want to wait for one of your kinfolk to go grab a rope from the golf cart so you can hang me?"

"You're overreacting," Reece said quietly. "This isn't a lynch mob."

"Could have fooled me," she shot back.

Mitch realized that his family and friends were all looking pissed enough to justify her accusation.

He took Belle's arm and pulled her away from the crowd, up toward the ninth hole where they could talk without all the commentary.

"Belle, tell me what's going on," he asked when they reached some semblance of privacy. "The truth this time."

"I told you the truth. You're choosing to believe that guy over me." She gestured to the photographer Reece was tossing into the golf cart. "You're so busy obsessing over your image, over your need to prove yourself perfect that you won't even consider that you're wrong."

Mitch bristled at the accusation. To hell with that. He wasn't trying to prove a damned thing. He was just protecting his investment. He recalled her reluctance to come down to the lake earlier. Had she been having second thoughts? Or had it been because her plans were derailed when they'd gotten the lakeside envelope? God, he was the world's biggest idiot.

"Is that what you think?" he asked. "That I'm obsessed with image? Well if I am, you sure blew it all to hell with this little stunt. Again," he accused. Mitch spared a glance at his family, here to watch another of his dreams smashed to hell.

Belle gave a bitter laugh and shook his hand off her arm. She took a step backward as if she couldn't stand to be close to him. Mitch wanted to grab her and yell that he wasn't the guilty party here. He'd be damned if she'd make him feel bad that she'd been busted at her own game.

"You go ahead and believe that," she said. "It's easier for you to blame me than figure out the truth." She gave a wave of her hand toward the crowd and swallowed, her jaw working and eyes blinking rapidly. "I thought I could trust you this time. I thought you were different. My God, I was such an idiot."

Spying her shoes on the grass, she leaned over and snatched them up, then tilted her chin at him. "There is no advantage to me ruining my own business reputation. There is no point in busting my ass to make this event, this entire themed resort, come together perfectly if I was going to just screw it all up in the end."

She stepped closer and punched her index finger into his chest. "Someone is fucking you over and it's not me. Why don't you grow up and quit flexing your dick and go find out who it really is?"

With that, she stomped up the hill toward the golf carts parked haphazardly all over the ninth hole.

Her words echoed in his head. His family's voices faded into background noise.

Brow furrowed, Mitch watched Belle slam the golf cart into gear and drive away. Part of him wanted to yell to her to wait. He wanted to run after her and fix things. But his family was all standing around. And they'd just seen Belle make him look like a loser idiot in front of them. Again. He let her go. Confusion and pain clawed at his gut. Belle had used him, used this event, all for publicity?

Once again, he'd lost the princess. And once again, he'd lost face in front of his entire family as she screwed him over.

Mitch tried to console himself that at least this time he'd had a whole bunch of hot, wild, kinky sex. But all that did was remind him of what he'd lost. Of what he'd never actually had.

Wasn't he a pitiful chump?

13

BELLE STUMBLED into her cottage, tears streaming down her face. She stopped cold when she was hit with a faceful of bright light and heavy metal music.

Damn. She'd forgotten Sierra would be there.

"You're back early," her friend yelled over Black Sabbath. "What happened? All that rocking the boat make you seasick?" She was one to tease, given that she was twisted around like a pretzel with her ass in the air.

"Paparazzi," Belle said shortly, not able to find her usual razz about Sierra being the only person in the world who practiced yoga to Ozzie. She scrubbed the tears off her face with the back of her hand.

Sierra fell sideways with a crash. "What?" she asked, rubbing her shoulder. She finally took a look at Belle's face and jumped up to slap the stereo off. "Oh, my God, what's wrong?"

"Paparazzi," Belle repeated, throwing her shoes across the room so hard they knocked a teacup off the table, sending it to a shattered death on the tile floor.

She glared at the mess, and not even caring that she was barefoot, stormed over to the couch. She dropped to the cushions, drew her knees up for comfort and waited.

She didn't have to wait long. Two seconds later and Sierra was right there, wrapping her arms around Belle. Belle took a shuddering breath, but before she could spill the details of the horrible encounter and Mitch's betrayal, someone pounded on her door.

"Belle, I want to talk to you."

Her body went numb at the sound of Mitch's voice. Sierra stood to answer the door but Belle grabbed her damp T-shirt and gave a shake of her head.

He pounded again.

"Now."

Her chin flew up and anger, drowned out earlier by her tears, rekindled.

Sierra took one look at her face and yelled back, "Get lost."

Silence.

Sierra gave a satisfied smirk, but Belle knew better. Ten seconds later the pounding started again. Confused, angry and hurt beyond belief, she still knew she had to face him. But not yet.

She went to the door and, after flicking off the overhead light to help hide her ravaged face, she set the security chain, then opened the door.

Mitch's fury was clear through the small opening. It was all she could do not to start crying again at the sight. Determined to cling to some form of dignity, she took a deep breath. Before he could say a word, she held up her hand. "I'll discuss the situation with you in a half hour," she told him. "I'm not dressed for this and I'm not prepared to talk to you yet."

"You're not negotiating a contract, Belle." The disdain in his voice was so sharp, she wondered if she'd be left with a scar.

She inclined her head toward him and gave a one-shouldered shrug. "No, but this is business, isn't it? If you want to talk tonight, I'll come up to your office in a half hour. Otherwise it will wait until tomorrow."

She watched his jaw work and knew he was struggling for control. His anger, so clear in the set of his shoulders and furious glare, shouldn't turn her on. But, sicko that she was, it did, just a little. Her heart whimpered at the uselessness of the realization.

"Fifteen minutes," he finally said.

"Thirty," she repeated.

He snarled and lifted his fist as if he were going to pound it through the door. But he didn't. Instead he growled, "Fine."

Belle didn't wait for him to leave. She shut the door and, knowing it would only add to his fury, flipped the locks with a loud snick.

She turned to see Sierra staring, the shock in her blue eyes echoed in her slack jaw.

"What?"

"Just wondering where you're hiding those brass balls. Your dress is awfully revealing."

Belle gave a watery laugh and collapsed against the door. Her fury-induced adrenaline washed away, leaving her limp and miserable.

"We're just getting hot and heavy on the dock and out jumps a blood-sucking photographer snapping pictures, calling dirty suggestions." Belle shivered at the memory. "It was horrible. Then, before I could take that in, up squeals Reece like the cavalry, grabbing the guy and beating the hell out of him."

Sierra's fascinated curiosity turned to derision and she shook her head. "Leave it to him to get all macho," she muttered. Then she glanced at the clock, grabbed Belle's arm and tugged her toward the bedroom.

"Talk while you're changing. We have twenty-five minutes."

"The paparazzi said it was me, the party girl," Belle whispered. "He said I'd hired him. Arranged all this."

Sierra sucked in a sharp breath. Then she let out a low, vicious growl that would do a momma cat proud. "Someone's setting you up."

Belle shrugged and started changing.

"And there was that smug-faced bitch, Lena Carter, just gloating over the whole ugly mess," Belle summed up as she finished recounting the horrible scene while reapplying foundation to cover her blotchy, tearstained skin.

"Lena Norris," Sierra corrected, her voice muffled by the sweater she was pulling over her head.

Belle lowered the makeup brush and stared at her friend's reflection. "What?"

Sierra settled the black cashmere sweater in place and pulled her hair free, then met Belle's eyes in the mirror. "Norris. She's not one of the Carter clan. I found out tonight when I read the guest list over Larry's shoulder."

She and Belle exchanged a long, comprehending stare.

"L.N.," they said together.

Stunned, Belle dropped her makeup brush on the counter and sank onto the wide edge of the spa tub. That nasty vindictive woman was behind all this?

"What a bitch." Sierra gave a little growl and shook her head. "I can't believe it. I thought she had it in for you, but it's actually her own brother she's been trying to screw over all these years."

Belle tugged on her short suede boots and considered the idea. God, she'd been a gullible idiot.

Six years ago she'd scurried away at the first sign of conflict instead of talking to Mitch or her father. As always, she'd been so sure she'd be rejected if she confronted the issue. Shame washed over her. Apparently she was a wimp as well as an idiot.

But not this time. She sucked in a deep, fortifying breath and squared her shoulders, trying to find courage. Hell, Mitch had already rejected her, so she had nothing left to lose. And one hell of a lot to gain by outing that obnoxious bitch, Lena.

"She's planning on ruining more than a wedding this time," Belle pointed out, anger making her hand shake as she tried to apply lip gloss. "Mitch's business is her goal this round."

Belle tried to focus on that, but she couldn't quite get over the indignity of being so easily manipulated. She wanted to beat the hell out of Lena. And not some girly slap-fight, either. She wanted to gut-punch the other woman.

"What a dirty sneak," she muttered.

"Exactly."

Belle let the fury of it all propel her out of the room. "C'mon," she called back to Sierra, who was hopping from foot to foot trying to put on her platforms. "I have to tell Mitch. As soon as he hears this, we can sit back and watch him deal with that duplicitous bitch."

Belle had never been one to contemplate revenge before, but suddenly the idea filled her with a grim satisfaction. She couldn't wait to see Lena pay for everything she'd done. To Mitch, to the resort. To Belle.

Five minutes early, Belle stormed into Mitch's office, Sierra hot on her heels. It was like walking into an ice-filled courtroom. Belle shivered, her momentum stalled at the implacable coldness on Mitch's face. Like a judge, he sat behind his desk, the position of power loud and clear.

There was a movement by the window and Belle's gaze shot to the prosecutor du jour. The fiery anger in Reece's glare was the only heat in the room. Nerves snapped and snarled in her stomach, the little voice in the back of her head warning her to give it up and run. Get the hell out of there before they verbally shredded her.

She'd actually taken a step back before she realized what she was doing. No. Belle squared her shoulders and forced herself to stand still. They wanted to judge, that was fine. She was here for justice.

Knowing the only way she'd get through this was to block Reece's intimidating presence out of her mind, Belle focused on Mitch. It took her two deep belly breaths to get the nerve, then she stomped over to his desk and slapped her hands on the surface.

It was a good indication of how angry he was when he kept his gaze locked on hers instead of letting it drop to the view highlighted by her low-cut blouse. *Okay, fine.* She told herself she wasn't worried that her one real weapon had already proved ineffective.

"Look, I know who's behind all your problems," she said quietly. His blank stare didn't change, but Belle pressed on. "Just hear me out and we'll get to the truth of this whole mess."

"Truth?" Mitch snapped. She winced as his frigid tone sliced at her. "Or excuses?"

Tears threatened again, but Belle blinked them away. She felt Sierra come up behind her. Her friend didn't say anything, just stood a little behind and off to the side, giving silent support. It was all Belle needed. With a deep breath, she handed Mitch the papers she'd found in Diana's office. He didn't look at them, just slid them aside and kept his eyes on hers. With a quick glance at Sierra, who nodded, she went on to describe how they'd searched through Diana's computer files.

Through it all, the men said nothing. Mitch just sat there, his hands steepled as he stared at her emotionlessly. Reece lounged against the windowsill, one cowboy boot tapping impatiently.

Finally, Reese straightened and walked toward the door. "You're accusing Diana?" he asked as he passed her.

"I found the information in her office," Belle shot back, her tone pissy and defensive. It was like they hadn't even heard what she said. She gave Reece the evil eye, to which he only raised a brow.

"We talked to her," Mitch said quietly. Belle glanced back at him. His face was still blank. Her fingers twitched nervously. She couldn't read him at all and it was starting to scare her. "Turns out you're right."

Belle opened her mouth to argue with him, then closed it. "Right?"

"She's not the mastermind, obviously. Diana's just a very good, very efficient assistant." She knew him well enough to recognize the betrayed hurt beneath his bitter words.

"Mitch, I'm sorry," Belle murmured.

Instead of accepting her sympathy, he just gave a snort of disbelief.

Belle's brows drew together.

Before she could say anything else, though, Reece opened the side door to the boardroom and gestured to a security guard on the other side.

Suddenly nervous but not sure why, Belle looked at Sierra. Her friend shot the security guard and his big gun a concerned look and rubbed a quick hand over the small of Belle's back in support.

But the only person to enter the room was unarmed. And, from the look of her, totally broken. Diana's hair, styled so carefully for the party, hung in a stringy curtain around her tear-ravaged face. She shot Belle a fearful look, then took the furthest seat away from everyone.

Reece sat opposite her, his long legs kicked out in front of him in a pose so relaxed it was a total insult to the situation. Belle wanted to beat him upside the cowboy hat with Mitch's desk blotter.

"Diana, you go ahead and repeat what you told Mitch and me earlier."

"I'd rather not," she mumbled into her lap.

"That's too bad," Mitch said shortly. "It's talk to us or talk to the cops. Take your pick."

She gave a deep, shuddering sort of sigh, then, twisting her hands together in a way that was painful to watch, started in a hesitant voice, "I told you already, I admit to helping sabotage Lakeside."

"On whose orders?" Mitch demanded.

The tension in Belle's shoulders loosened, anticipation and a weird sort of vindication surging through her. Yes, now Lena would get what was coming to her.

"Hers," Diana mumbled, the word so quiet they all had to lean forward to hear it.

Sierra and Belle exchanged confused looks.

"You mean Belle?" Reece asked in a low, empty tone.

"What?" Belle couldn't believe the question.

"Yes," Diana whispered.

The room tilted just a little and Belle felt her stomach pitch. "You're so lying. I didn't do a damned thing."

Diana just shrugged. Reece took off his cowboy hat and ran the brim through his fingers before putting it back on. Belle's gaze, filled with confusion and panic, flew to Mitch. He didn't believe this crap, did he?

He stared back at her, his eyes steady and furious.

Apparently he found the crap perfectly believable.

Her heart cracked, tiny tentacles of pain radiating through her system. She should have known. She never should have let herself feel anything for him. Tears burned the backs of her eyes as she tried to figure out why Diana would tell such lies. And more importantly, how Mitch could so easily believe them.

"Since when did you start taking orders from Belle?" Sierra snapped.

Diana gave a helpless little shrug, her gaze locked on her toes. "Since she offered me a job with her father's hotels."

Belle's gasp drowned out Sierra's hiss at the lie.

Showing the first spark since she'd come slinking into the room, Diana ignored them and threw an accusing look at Mitch before continuing. "She promised me her father runs a normal office. I'd be managing a successful hotel, not ordering disgusting sex toys."

Belle narrowed her eyes. "The sabotage was happening long before I showed up with my disgusting sex ideas."

Diana gave a tiny smirk and inclined her head. "That was the plan, wasn't it? And why I pushed your business so hard when you lured away the last event planner."

Belle stared in shock. "Oh my God, you don't really think they're going to believe this, do you? You are sitting there telling straight-up lies and you think you can get away with it?"

"Why would I lie?" Diana countered. The look in her eyes made Belle realize that this little mouse had sharp teeth and deadly claws. "I'm already being brought up on charges. I've lost my job, my reputation and, since you blew it, I'm sure I've lost all the recompense you promised me, too."

"I didn't promise you a damned thing," Belle growled, her hands fisted on her hips.

"Did you have contact with Diana before you came to Lakeside?" Reece asked.

"Of course." Before she could explain that it had been Diana who'd contacted Eventfully Yours for the job, Reece continued.

"Did you come to Lakeside for any purpose other than to secure a job contract?"

How could she answer that? If she admitted she'd come for her father, they'd only see it as more guilt. But she couldn't lie, either. Belle wet her lips.

"Did you?" Mitch asked quietly.

"I, well, yes, I had other reasons. Mitch and I had a history. I wanted to see him again."

Reece's passive demeanor cracked just a little, showing a hint of derision. "Really? The man you left at the altar? You had a sudden hankering to what? Stroll down memory lane?"

"Of course not," Belle said with a scowl. "We had unfinished business. I wanted to see Mitch," she looked at her ex-fiancé and shrugged. "I tried to see you a couple of times before, but never got past first base. We had stuff to talk about, a past to deal with."

Belle tried to find the words to apologize for running off on him, for the humiliation and devastation of leaving him at the altar. But there were too many people in the room, too much nastiness going on. Instead she just shrugged.

"So you admit it," Reece said. "You had motive, means and opportunity before you showed up here."

"Oh. My. God," Sierra snapped. "What is this, a bad Sherlock Holmes novel? Get a magnifying glass or get over yourself."

"I had an apology to make," Belle said softly. She saw Mitch's eyes widen in surprise and wanted to scream with frustration. What? Did he think her so much a bitch that she'd have no regret about what had happened?

Belle pressed her lips together. With every fiber of her being, she wanted to throw her hands in the air and say screw it. To walk—no run—out of the office and escape this nasty scene. Then her gaze fell on Mitch. Beneath the palpable fury emanating from him she saw something else. Pain.

Tears, so easily held at bay for herself, welled up for him. Regardless of how she felt about the unfounded accusations, the ugly mistrust and rotten character assessment, the bottom line was he was the one being hurt.

And she was the one being used to hurt him. She needed to focus on that, to let it excuse his actions. But as much as she tried, she couldn't. The truth was he didn't trust her. And without trust, they were nothing but fuck buddies.

"This is the second accusation thrown at me tonight," she said quietly through the pain of her realization. "Both of them are complete and total bullshit. If you knew me at all, if the last few weeks we've spent together had meant a damned thing to you, you'd know they were bullshit."

Belle stepped away from the desk and, because she was suddenly freezing, wrapped her arms around herself and shook her head at Mitch. "But you're too busy worrying about your image. The only thing that matters to you is that people think you're Mr. Perfect, that your family holds you on some stupid pedestal."

His fist clenched on the desk, Mitch didn't say anything.

Fury driving her words, Belle continued to spew uncontrollably. "The fact that it makes no sense doesn't seem to matter to you and your vigilante cowboy here. If I wanted to screw you over, there are a dozen ways. None of them include busting my butt to create and implement a creative and unique hook to help you succeed."

Belle shoved a hand through her hair and saw it was shaking. Hell, her entire body was shaking, she was so upset. Her breath came in gasps now, her vision blurred around the edges.

"If you want to blame me, you have a good ol' time with it. But the person you should be looking at is your sister." Even through her pain, Belle winced at the raw delivery and its effect on Mitch. His face paled, his mouth dropped open. All in all, he looked as though she'd just kicked him in the 'nads.

Oh God, look what confrontation got her. A big fat lot of pain and misery. She hadn't changed their minds about a damned thing, and now she'd hurt him. Belle pressed her hand to her mouth to hold back a scream of frustration and shook her head.

"I can't do this. You go ahead and believe whatever you want. If it helps to make me the culprit here, go ahead. I'll send you my lawyer's name. We'll deal with it that way." She had to get out of the room. She could barely breathe through all the tension and pain pounding in her chest.

She felt Sierra's arm on her shoulder and leaned in, needing the support of at least one person in the room. She drew strength from her friend, then straightened and gave Mitch a long, clear look.

"You're right, though. I wasn't completely honest with you. I did show up here hoping for more than a contract from you. I came here hoping you'd talk with my father. Give him some advice and ideas." She felt like a traitor admitting her self-serving motivation, but figured the truth couldn't be anywhere near as debilitating as the crap they were making up.

"But once I got here, once I got to know you again—no," she corrected, "got to know you period, then my reasons changed. All I wanted was to see you succeed, Mitch. To see the resort succeed."

Behind her, Diana gave a watery snort. Belle spun around, not sure if she was going to scream at the bitch or beat the hell out of her. Before she could do either, though, Sierra launched herself past Belle, claws outstretched.

Diana squealed and jumped back, lifting her feet into the seat with her as she tried to curl up in a ball.

Reece grabbed Sierra around the waist and swung her away from the whimpering traitor.

Belle's nerves were jangling and raw at the violence, both in the room, and churning inside her.

Mitch just sat there watching, his face impassive.

"You don't believe her, do you?" she asked, her words barely discernible as Sierra screamed obscenities at Diana and Reece tried to calm her.

"I don't like being used," Mitch finally said as Reece and Sierra's swearing died down.

The implied accusation tore her heart in two.

"You're one to talk," Belle sobbed. Finally unable to hold back the one ugly truth that had eaten at her heart for more than six years, she said, "When have you done anything but use me?"

Saying the words aloud was like opening Pandora's box. Pain, misery and a million and one self-doubts all came flying out at her. Vicious and biting, they ripped at her. The look on Mitch's face, judgmental and angry, proved that she'd never stood a chance.

Belle tried to speak, but her throat was constricted with tears. She just shook her head and turned away.

It wasn't until Reece handed her a handkerchief on her way out the door that she realized she had tears dripping off her chin.

14

MITCH WATCHED Reece escort Belle into the foyer of the hotel, his heart stuttering a little at how gorgeous she was in the morning light. Apparently she took the phrase *dress to kill* seriously. A short, fitted skirt hugged hips his fingers itched to hold and her blouse wrapped around her torso enticingly, highlighting her cleavage. Power heels in a kick-your-ass red completed the look.

Her face was set, like a beautiful ice carving. Her eyes, though, sparkled with fiery anger. God, he loved her. His gut hurt at the idea of how much pain he'd caused her last night. As soon as she'd left, he'd told Reece it was a set-up. He was sure of it. Despite the mountain of proof Diana had offered—e-mails, faxes, Belle's signature on everything, he knew she hadn't done it.

Starting with the papers Belle had left him, they'd spent the entire night digging for the answer. An answer that had hurt like crazy but one that Mitch knew was true.

Now all he had to find out was why. And that, he figured, Belle had a right to know, too.

As they reached him, he murmured his thanks to Reece, who nodded and tilted his head to indicate that he'd be waiting in the restaurant.

"How fun. We've gone from unsubstantiated accusations to goon patrol?" Belle commented, giving him a dirty look.

"Am I so worthless that you can't just come talk to me directly? You need to send your big security chief to fetch my criminal butt?"

Mitch opened his mouth to explain, but one of his aunts walked past just then and yelled an enthusiastic hello. He grimaced and shut his mouth again. He'd almost blown it. This was too important to screw up with a lame explanation. He had to show her. To show her and his entire family that Belle was innocent.

Belle frowned in confusion when he didn't say anything. Then she glanced at his departing aunt and got one of those you-are-such-a-pig looks on her face. "Oooh, I get it. I have cooties. You need to distance yourself from me so you don't tilt any further off that precarious pedestal you're perched on."

Even though he knew he was being a jerk and that she had every right to be angry, Mitch couldn't stop from giving her a narrow-eyed look and asking, "Alliteration so early in the day?"

Anger spat from her sea-green eyes and her mouth thinned. She looked like she was going to slug him. Mitch realized he was a sick puppy when the idea turned him on. God, he had it bad when any sign of passion from her, even non-sexual, got him all hot and horny.

"Let's walk," he suggested.

"Let's not," she returned. "You were too rude to talk to me privately before I'm escorted off the premises, so you can tell me what you want right here."

Mitch grinned and took her arm to pull her to his side. Yeah, she was one helluva turn-on. "C'mon, I'll show you."

Her fury was clear in the snap of her heels against the floor and the stiff set of her shoulders. Of course, the sharp elbow in his gut was a good indicator, too.

But she didn't pull away as he escorted her into the packed restaurant. She hesitated in the entrance, her step hitching just a little. Realizing she must think he was furthering that public-lynching thing she'd accused him of last night, Mitch shifted his hold, releasing her arm to wrap his hand around her waist.

Her accusation about him using her echoed in his head. Had been echoing through the long night. She was right and he hated himself for that. He'd hoped that publicly vindicating her would start to make up for his previous dicklessness, but once again, he'd miscalculated.

"It'll be fine," he whispered. He knew Reece wanted the element of surprise on their side. That for the trap to work hinged on Belle's unscripted reactions. But he couldn't stand seeing her suffer. If it meant only that he, Reece and the culprit knew the real truth, that was fine. He realized he didn't want the public vindication at the cost of Belle's feelings.

"Look, let's go to my office," he said softly, watching the nerves play over her features at the sight of his entire clan gathered in the dining room. The need to protect her overwhelmed him. Whispers carried around the room, fingers pointed and angry looks flew at Belle. Mitch shot a blanket glare at everyone.

He'd been a total idiot to give in to Reece's plan. All he'd thought of was to publicly prove Belle's innocence. To push Lena to admit in front of everyone here that she was behind the problems. Not to vindicate himself, but so nobody, ever, could doubt Belle again. He hadn't thought the scheme through enough to realize what she'd have to endure in the process, though.

"Let's go," he repeated. "We'll talk there."

Some of the tension left her body as she leaned into him just a bit. She started to nod. Then something, or someone, caught her eye and she went steel-straight again and gave a little growl under her breath.

"That *bitch* is eating my afterglow special?" she asked.

Mitch followed her gaze and pulled a face. He glanced at

Reece, seated across the room at the table next to the afterglow special, and grimaced.

Guess the show was still on. Belle pulled away with a hiss and stalked across the dining room. Yep, show on, whether he wanted it to be or not. He shoved his hands into his pockets and, body tensing for battle, followed her across the room.

Belle, apparently the consummate hostess even when blinded by spitting fury, sidestepped his family's snide comments and rude questions graciously. But she didn't slow down.

Thankfully his legs were longer, so, by the time she reached Lena's table, Mitch had caught up. Mitch joined her as she sat, uninvited, at the damask-covered table.

"Lena," he greeted quietly. He watched his stepsister's eyes, knowing they gave the only clue to what was really going on behind that wide forehead of hers. They showed curiosity. He had to admire her. She was so damned sure she'd won, she didn't feel a speck of fear.

"I realize it's a public restaurant, so to speak," Lena said in a haughty tone, "but I think I have the right to enjoy my breakfast without being interrupted by a traitorous sex-peddler."

Mitch glanced out the dining-room window at the gorgeous view of his beloved woods. The woods that had made him buy this property. The ones that made him feel like he'd finally made it. The woods where he'd been made to look like a loser idiot. And not, he knew, turning his gaze to Belle, by the woman he loved.

No, he had family to thank for that.

"I'll give you sex—" Belle started to rage, leaning across the table.

"Really, Lena?" he interrupted, laying a hand on Belle's knee. She shot him a furious look. Her anger turned to confusion when his eyes asked her to trust him. He was asking for the moon, he knew. That, the sun and a few planets, given that all he'd ever done was betray her.

But damned if she didn't give it anyway. With a tiny furrow of her brow, she gave an infinitesimal nod and released her breath.

"I'm surprised you can sit there eating like you haven't a care in the world," he continued, gesturing to her almost-empty plate as well as the two side dishes she'd apparently enjoyed. "Are you so sure of yourself that you aren't the least bit worried?"

Lena scooped up a bite of strawberry mousse and gestured with her spoon. "I haven't done anything wrong. Although I've been hearing whispers from your staff, one of your cute security guys to be precise, that the same can't be said for everyone at this table."

Belle looked positively feral and Mitch decided he didn't want to play the game. Unable to keep the hurt and anger from his voice, he leaned across the table and asked quietly, "Why'd you do it, Lena? Why'd you try and sabotage my resort?"

At Belle's loud gasp, the few people that weren't already watching the tableau looked their way. Her hand covered his where it lay on her knee and squeezed. Satisfaction and a spark of hope that she might forgive him sprang to life in Mitch's heart.

"What'd she do, screw you stupid?" Lena shot back.

Belle surged out of her chair so fast, it toppled over. But she wasn't as fast as Mitch or Reece.

Mitch was around the table before Belle's chair hit the floor, grabbing his stepsister by the arm and pulling her to her feet. Reece put his hand on Belle's arm, probably worried she'd resort to the same type of violence Sierra had tried the night before.

"As always, she's a public embarrassment to you, isn't she, Mitch?" Lena mocked.

"Kiss my ass," Belle suggested sweetly. But Mitch could see the pain the comment had caused in Belle's eyes.

"Oh, please," Lena snapped. "I don't know what kind of

game she's playing, but this is ridiculous. She's making a fool of you with your entire family as witnesses. Again. Keep this up and nobody's going to have to wonder if they should doubt your judgment or not. They'll know you've let them all down."

He had to hand it to her, she definitely knew where to twist the knife. Mitch saw a movement out of the corner of his eye and winced when he recognized the straw purse. Grammy Lynn had joined them. Good. He didn't want one single person missing the proof that Belle was innocent.

"You know, the funny thing about computer messages is that even though you can fake an e-mail address, you can't fake an IP address," Mitch said quietly. "And that paparazzi you hired? He's the kind of guy who ignores orders to delete phone records. You—or Diana—covered your asses when you made the calls from the resort. But those text messages you sent him last night? They traced right back to your cell phone, Lena. It was a clever plan. But not clever enough."

His stepsister hissed and wrenched her arm away. With a glare of hatred, she said, "You're just Mr. Golden Boy, aren't you? You think you're so perfect. Everything just falls into your lap. You deserve all these problems. These and more."

"You're such a nasty bitch," Belle accused in a shocked whisper.

"And you're an interfering one. I was this close," she spat, holding her fingers in front of Belle's face, "to winning. You just lucked out, that's all."

Mitch gave Reece a look, and in an instant his cousin had switched places with him. Now Reece had Lena cornered, leaving Mitch free to put his arm around Belle's shoulder.

"No. Even without proof, I knew Belle wasn't behind this."

"How?" Belle asked quietly beside him.

He looked down into her face, her beautiful green eyes glistening with tears and happiness. Mitch's heart shifted, all the worries and fear dropping away as he leaned down to brush a soft kiss over her full lips.

"Because I trust you."

"I WANTED to smack you silly when I first saw you this morning," Belle murmured to Mitch an hour later. After the big show and resulting fallout, she and Sierra had watched gleefully from the sidelines as Lena was hauled off the property by the cops.

Now, an hour later, she and Mitch had escaped to the serenity of the woods for a "picnic" and a talk. She'd rather picnic than talk, but he'd told her to keep her clothes on until he'd said his piece.

Then he'd proceeded to pull her down on the blanket and kiss her silly instead of talking.

"I could tell you were eyeing me like a punching bag," he acknowledged against her hair. His chest shook as he laughed silently. "Don't actually hit me when I tell you this, but it was a total turn-on seeing you that pissed. I wanted to strip you naked and do you on the registration desk."

She pulled back to look at his face and laugh, then she shook her head. "Crazy. You're absolutely crazy."

"I can't help it. It drives me nuts when you get all confrontational."

Belle ducked her head back onto his chest to hide her tears. The one thing she'd always been so afraid of and Mitch loved it. A bubbling kind of joy burst inside her, sending sparks of happiness through her system. Belle wanted to laugh and cry and dance around wildly. She swallowed, not willing to cry all over him again. Apparently she was free to hit him, though.

A beautiful sense of peace washed over her. She had no idea where they were going from here, especially since her contract with the resort would be fulfilled by the end of the month. But she did know she was holding tight to Mitch, and hey, if she wanted to get in his face about any issues that came up, she'd just been green-lighted.

Still giggling at the idea of her aggression being a turn-on, she wondered if the registration area was ever completely private. Belle snuggled deeper into his arms and sighed as she watched the breeze dance through the canopy of leaves overhead.

After a few more idyllic minutes in his arms, though, Belle started squirming. All this cuddling stuff was sweet, but she wanted her picnic.

"I'm still waiting to hear your *piece,*" she finally reminded him. "If you'd get on with it, we could move on with this afternoon's entertainment."

Mitch laughed and hugged her even tighter.

"Why'd she do it?" she asked quietly, afraid to ruin the tranquility of the moment but needing to know.

"Money. Apparently she was livid that her father willed his company to me. He'd left her a small fortune, but she thought she should have gotten more. She saw his leaving me anything as a betrayal. She said that's why she refused to sit on the board, to have anything to do with me. She's partnered up with a rival developer and I guess she figured when I tanked here, she'd swoop in and buy the place cheap."

"Crazy," Belle breathed. "She really thought that would work?"

Mitch's shirt rubbed softly against her cheek as he shrugged. "She had the financial backing. Real estate is plummeting and she's got the inside track. Hell, if her plan had worked instead of us…you…catching her, I'd have probably thanked Lena for bailing me out."

"That's like saying if pigs could fly then Manolos would fall from the sky," Belle scoffed. Mitch's brows drew together as he tried to decipher that, but she kept going before he could ask. "Her plan couldn't have worked. At best, it was an annoyance.

A pain in your butt and a crash test in 'what could go wrong' for the resort."

"Sure, now," he agreed. "But you read the list. Hell, you found it. She was saving the big guns for after the resort was actually open to the public."

"What's going to happen to her?" Belle asked quietly.

"We'll press charges. I don't want her jailed or anything, but Reece pointed out that we need to take legal steps just in case she tries something in the future."

She could tell he was beating himself up over it all. Determined not to let Lena leave a nasty aftertaste, Belle pushed the issue.

"You didn't do anything wrong. You're a success for a good reason, Mitch. You bust your ass, you're a brilliant strategist and, like my daddy always said, you have the touch. She couldn't have hurt the resort. Not really."

Belle bit her lip after saying that. While she thought of his hurt as having to do with business, maybe Mitch was suffering emotionally. After all, family was everything to him. "I'm sorry she hurt you, though," Belle added softly.

Mitch's eyes, so hard and irritated a second ago, melted to that soft, sexy cinnamon that she loved so much. He shook his head and grimaced. "She didn't hurt me so much as she slapped at my pride." He took a deep breath that made his chest do yummy things against Belle's breasts and shrugged. "It was bad enough her gunning for me. I mean, yes, her thinking was twisted, but there is some justification in her anger that I took her father's business and not only made it mine but brought my entire family on board and left her out in the cold."

"A cold she chose." Belle repeated what Reece had told her earlier. "You offered her a board position. She's the one who turned her nose up as if it wasn't good enough for her."

As Mitch considered her words, some of the tension left his shoulders. Then he nodded and told her, "She never really connected with my family. Grammy Lynn said it was because she was a snob and we weren't upscale enough. I just figured she felt left out."

Then his expression hardened. "But as much as I might try and understand her reasons for aiming at me, there is no excuse for her trying to incriminate you."

Belle searched herself, but there wasn't any anger left. The sight of Lena's arrogant ass being hauled off in handcuffs had satisfied her need for revenge. Not wanting to waste any more time on Lena or her twisted motives, Belle shifted just a little so her breasts brushed Mitch's chest. Smart man that he was, he slid one hand inside her blouse to cup her, his fingers doing a soft, easy swirl around her hardening nipple.

"No matter, it's done," Belle said, angling her bent leg over Mitch's thighs so she could feel his erection hardening. "She doesn't matter, she's finished. We're not, though."

"And that's what counts," Mitch said with satisfaction.

Their lips met in a kiss that scared the hell out of Belle. Not because of the intensity of it, but because of the sweetness. She could so get addicted to this kind of kissing. It felt like the promise of forever.

"By the way," Mitch said as he curled his fingers through hers and lifted her hand to his lips, "I talked to your father this morning."

Nothing said *cold shower* on an intimate moment louder than the mention of a parent. Belle automatically tugged her blouse into place and shifted just a little so she wasn't pressed against his erection.

"Daddy?" she asked with a confused frown. "Why?"

"I didn't realize until Reece did some digging that your father was in a financial mess, in part because of that property we'd planned to develop. Although he did say that you'd done a fine job of bailing him out of most of his problems."

Belle blushed at the impressed smile he gave her, but didn't say anything. She wanted to know why he'd called her father. More importantly, she wanted to know how the two most important men in her life had gotten along.

"Your dad and I are meeting next week. Apparently we already have a dinner date," he said, giving her a teasing look. "We're going to go ahead with our original plans and develop that property."

Belle had to forcibly refrain from clapping her hands and cheering. She did grin, though, and gave Mitch a tight hug. When she pulled back, she noticed a look in his cinnamon-brown eyes. Dark, intense, direct. It scared the hell out of her. She swallowed. She'd promised herself the days of avoidance were a thing of the past, so instead of distracting him with sex, she asked, "What else? You look like there's something important you want to say."

He gave a snort of laughter and nodded. Then, her hand still in his, he kissed her palm and held their entwined hands against his heart.

"Through everything that's happened, you've believed in me, Belle. I've spent most of my life trying to prove myself, wanting to impress people. But you never needed proof and were impressed despite my mistakes." He looked deep into her eyes and sighed.

"Belle, I love you. I've always loved you, even if I wasn't smart enough to know it. I wanted to marry you six years ago for a million reasons. But love was definitely one of them."

Joy spun through her system so fast she was dizzy with it. Her laughter rang through the trees as she pulled her hand free so she could hug him close. Her body pressed against his, Belle could feel the beat of his heart and gave a giddy thanks, knowing it belonged to her.

"I love you, too," she said softly, pulling back to smile into his eyes. "I love everything about you. Your ambition and drive, your integrity, your devotion to your family. I love your sense of humor and how freaking incredible you are in bed. I just love you, Mitch."

He gave her a huge grin. "Good. Then you'll say yes."

"Sure," she agreed. Then her brows drew together and she shook her head. "Yes to what?"

He carefully rolled aside and reached around to the picnic basket. Pulling a medium-size package out, he handed the festively wrapped box to her and motioned that she should open it.

Lecturing herself for wishing it was a smaller, jewelry-sized box, Belle leaned on one elbow and tugged at the bow. With an excited laugh and a questioning glance, she pulled the lid off the box.

Her jaw dropped as tears filled her eyes.

"Oh, Mitch," she breathed.

Blinking furiously, she pulled out a pair of tennis shoes.

"I want to make sure you have a choice. Six years ago, I wanted to marry you for a million reasons," he repeated. "This time, I only want to marry you for one. The only reason that matters. I love you."

Belle wiped away the tears. She'd be damned if she'd be a weepy mess for the most incredible moment of her life. The man she'd been dreaming of forever, her perfect hero, was being all gushy and she wanted to enjoy every wonderful moment of it.

"Forever?" she asked.

"Forever."

With a cheek-splitting grin, she handed him back the tennis shoes and shook her head. "Then I won't be needing these, will I?"

* * * * *

*Celebrate 60 years of pure
reading pleasure with Harlequin®!*

*Step back in time and enjoy a sneak preview of an
exciting anthology from Harlequin® Historical with*
THE DIAMONDS OF WELBOURNE MANOR

This compelling anthology features three stories about
the outrageous Fitzmanning sisters. Meet Annalise, who
is never at a loss for words… But that can change with
an unexpected encounter in the forest.

*Available May 2009
from Harlequin® Historical.*

"I'm the illegitimate daughter of notoriously scandalous parents, Mr. Milford. Candidates for my hand are unlikely to be lining up at the gates."

"Don't be so quick to discount your charms, my dear. Or the charm of your substantial dowry. Or even your brothers' influence. There are as many reasons to marry as there are marriages."

Annalise snorted. "Oh, yes. Perhaps I shall marry for dynastic reasons, or perhaps for property or influence. After all, a loveless, practical marriage worked out so well for my mother."

"Well, you've routed me on that one. I can think of no suitable rejoinder." Ned rose to his feet and extended his hand. "And since that is the case, let me be the first to wish you a long and happy spinsterhood."

Her mouth gaped open. And then she laughed.

And he froze.

This was the first time, Ned realized. The first time he'd seen her eyes light up and her mouth curl. The first time he'd witnessed her features melded together in glorious accord to produce exquisite beauty.

Unbelievable what a change came over her face. Unheard of

what effect her throaty, rasping laughter had on his body. It pounded a beat upon his ear, quickly taken up by his pulse. It echoed through him, finally residing in his stirring nether regions.

So easily she did it, awakened these sensations within him—without any apparent effort at all. And she had called him potentially dangerous? Clearly the intelligent thing for him to do would be to steer clear, to leave her to the tender ministrations of Lord Peter Blackthorne.

"You were right." She smiled up at him as she took his hand and climbed to her feet. "I do feel better."

Ah, well. When had he ever chosen the intelligent path?

He did not relinquish her hand. He used it to pull her in, close enough that he could feel the warmth of her. "At the risk of repeating Lord Peter's mistake and anticipating too much—may I ask if you'll be my partner in battledore tomorrow?"

Her smiled dimmed. Her breath came a little faster. His own had gone shallow, as if he'd just run a race—and lost. He ran his gaze over the appealing lift of her brow and the curious angle of her chin. His index finger twitched.

"I should like that," she said.

His finger trembled again and he lifted it, traced the pink and tender shell of her ear, the unique sweep of her jaw. Her pulse leaped beneath her skin, triggering his own. Slowly he tilted her chin up, waiting for her to object, to step back, to slap his hand away.

She did none of those eminently sensible things. Which left him free to do the entirely impractical thing.

Baby soft, the skin of her lips. Her whole body trembled when he touched her there.

He leaned in. Her eyes closed, even as she stood straight against him, strung as tight as a bow. He pressed his mouth to hers. It was a soft kiss, sweet and chaste. And yet he was hot and hard and as ready as he'd ever been in his life.

She drew back a little. Sighed. Their breath mingled a moment before she slowly backed away.

"Oh," she breathed. Her dark eyes were full of wonder and something that looked like fear. He took a step toward her, but she only shook her head. His outstretched hand fell to his side as she turned to disappear into the wood. This was the first time, Ned realized. The first time, since he'd come to the house party at Welbourne Manor, that he'd seen her eyes light up.

* * * * *

Follow Ned and Annalise's story in May 2009 in
THE DIAMONDS OF WELBOURNE MANOR
Available May 2009
from Harlequin® Historical

Available in the series romance section,
or in the historical romance section,
wherever books are sold.

**We'll be spotlighting a different series
every month throughout 2009
to celebrate our 60th anniversary.**

Look for Harlequin® Historical in May!

**60 years of Harlequin,
600 years of romance
in Harlequin Historical!**

www.eHarlequin.com   HHBPA09

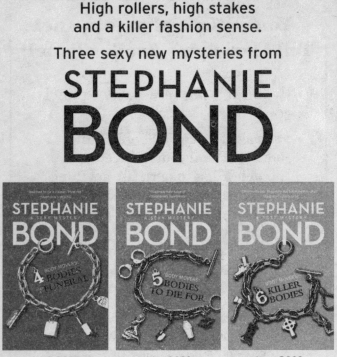

Silhouette® Desire

MAN of the MONTH

LEANNE BANKS

BILLIONAIRE EXTRAORDINAIRE

Billionaire Damien Medici is determined to get revenge on his enemy, but his buttoned-up new assistant Emma Weatherfield has been assigned to spy on him and might thwart his plans. As tensions in and out of the boardroom heat up, he convinces her to give him the information he needs—by getting her to unbutton a few things....

Available May
wherever books are sold.

Harlequin® Historical
Historical Romantic Adventure!

If you enjoyed reading
Joanne Rock in the
Harlequin® Blaze™ series,
look for her new book
from Harlequin® Historical!

THE KNIGHT'S RETURN
Joanne Rock

Missing more than his memory,
Hugh de Montagne sets out to find his
true identity. When he lands in a small
Irish kingdom and finds a new liege in the
Irish king, his hands are full with his new
assignment: guarding the king's beautiful,
exiled daughter. Sorcha has had her heart
broken by a knight in the past. Will she be
able to open her heart to love again?

Available April
wherever books are sold.